"I'll

In a flash Derrick was off the sofa, and with two steps in her direction, he reached down and pulled Noelle from the loveseat. His large hands fastened on her hips and moved her forward in one swoop until they were standing, pressed body to body.

Before Noelle's brain had time to even process, he was kissing her. And much to her amazement, she was kissing him back.

Oh, he tasted good! Like a cinnamon bun, Noelle thought dreamily, even as she parted her lips and allowed his warm tongue inside. Of their own volition, her arms slid up and over his broad shoulders, and she discovered he was just the right height for her to rest comfortably against him.

Noelle was not able to resist the soft sigh that escaped from her mouth. His tongue darted out and ran over her bottom lip in a slow, sensual caress, and Noelle felt her knees weaken.

But his strong hands tightly gathered the material of her skirt at each hip, holding her up and against him. She couldn't have fallen if she wanted to. Feeling the growing warmth pressing against her center, Noelle knew she should end the kiss, end the touching. This was wrong…so wrong.

But all she could do was allow her head to fall back as his soft lips left a trail of kisses from her chin to her collarbone. Her heartbeat sped up as she felt him grinding his growing erection against her. She couldn't have lied to herself if she wanted to. The feeling was mutual and she spontaneously began to meet his grind with her own.

Books by Elaine Overton

Kimani Romance

Fever
Daring Devotion
His Holiday Bride
Seducing the Matchmaker

Kimani Arabesque

Promises of the Heart
Déjà Vu
Love's Inferno

ELAINE OVERTON

currently resides in the Detroit area with her son and dog. She attended a local business college before entering the military and serving in the Gulf War. She is an administrative assistant, and currently works for an automotive industry supplier. She is also an active member of Romance Writers of America. You can contact her via e-mail at www.elaineoverton.com.

Seducing
the matchmaker

elaine overton

KIMANI
ROMANCE

To the Creator of all that is good in my life.
Thank you! Thank you! Thank you!

1 Thessalonians 5:16–18
Rejoice evermore.
Pray without ceasing.
In everything give thanks; for this is the will
of God in Christ Jesus concerning you.

 KIMANI PRESS™

ISBN-13: 978-0-373-86089-0
ISBN-10:   0-373-86089-7

SEDUCING THE MATCHMAKER

Copyright © 2008 by Elaine Overton

www.kimanipress.com

Printed in U.S.A.

Dear Reader,

Thank you for taking the time to read *Seducing the Matchmaker*. I hope you have enjoyed Derrick and Noelle's long, winding road toward a loving, open relationship.

Like most authors, I spend the majority of my writing time not actually putting words to paper but trying to show the reader what I see in my head. To me the characters are these fully formed, complicated people with lives and histories, and I want to share those stories with you, the way I *think* of them.

As a longtime romance reader, there is nothing I love better than the iconic diamond-in-the-rough, tortured hero and his journey to find a woman capable of loving ALL of him. I like to think of Derrick as just such a hero.

Noelle, who had her own hurdles to climb over— including her fear of emotional pain and her preoccupation with logic and reason—was still finally able to give her heart what it most desired. I think of her as the epitome of the old adage that sometimes what you want is not what you need.

I hope I did a fair job of explaining Derrick's troubled background and the events that forged his character, as well as Noelle's reasons behind her doubts. Now I would love to hear what *you* think, so feel free to write me at elaine@elaineoverton.com.

Take care,

Elaine

Chapter 1

Early December in Philadelphia, PA
Shortly after the first snow...

"I know what you must be thinking, Mr. Brandt."

I doubt that, Derrick Brandt thought, sitting in one of the comfortable, overstuffed guest chairs facing the neatly organized desk that belonged to Noelle Brown, the owner of Love Unlimited, a small but successful matchmaking service.

"You're thinking, why Love Unlimited and not one of the more popular online dating agencies? I have three words for you." She lifted three elegantly shaped fingers. "The personal touch. That one-on-one human contact that simply cannot be determined with questionnaires and evaluations. It's been my experience that any long-term relationship is only forty percent chemistry and sixty percent compatibility. And if the chemistry is right, it's instantaneous. So, that leaves the other sixty percent."

All the while she spoke, Derrick struggled to keep his eyes above the low-cut neckline of her mint-green silk blouse. He unconsciously licked his lips, imagining the bountiful treasure that lay just beneath the thin material. Try as he might, he simply could not help himself as his eyes repeatedly drifted south. She was so wonderfully endowed, and he was such a devoted breast man.

"Our methods are not always what one would consider traditional." She stretched her body to reach behind her chair and around to the credenza. Derrick allowed his hungry eyes to roam over her taut outline. Although the rest of her was hidden behind the desk, he already knew she was mostly legs. Long legs he could wrap around his waist. When she'd greeted him in the office lobby, his first impression had been of a luscious Amazon.

"But sometimes, finding just the right match takes something more than the conventional resources." She placed a brochure on the desk in front of him. "As you can see, we offer complete customer satisfaction."

She leaned forward to open the brochure, and the innocuous action thrust her bust up and outward in an irresistibly tempting display. "If we are unable to find a match for you within six months, you get an additional six months free. Fair enough?"

Derrick nodded mindlessly. The sum of his cognitive abilities was suddenly otherwise directed—riveted actually—on the lush brown mounds presented before him. The smooth, velvety, flawless skin was as rich and creamy as a cup of hot cocoa on a cold winter day.

If he leaned forward just a little, he could cup them in his hands. He could lift them to his face. He could inhale her decadent perfume. He could run his tongue over every curve and contour. Even through the thin silk material of her blouse, he could suck her into his mouth—

"We want the same thing."

Guiltily, his eyes shot up to her face.

"To find the right woman for you," she continued blithely. "And if you allow me to do what I do best, I will do exactly that. Do you have any questions?"

Derrick had questions all right. Was she a moaner or a screamer? The thought brought to mind images so provocative he felt the stirring of desire from his brain to the lap of his trousers. A lot of the men he knew were attracted to the petite, insanely thin women who graced magazine covers and television ads, but Derrick had always preferred the more robust, more Rubenesque female body.

While his buddies were drooling over Halle Berry, he was having wet dreams about Queen Latifah. He shifted in his chair, trying to hide his growing erection.

"Mr. Brandt?"

Derrick swallowed hard and tried to bring his mind back to the matter at hand. "No, no questions." He cleared his throat loudly. "So, what do I have to do to get started?"

"Well, first I need to get some basic information." She reached into a desk drawer and pulled out a file. "Just a short interview to give me a better understanding of the qualities you feel are most important."

She clicked her retractable pen and opened the file. "Let's start with physical attributes. What do you find attractive in a woman?"

"Large breasts."

Derrick watched as she scribbled rapid notes in the file. "Okay, anything else?"

"She needs to be a good breeder."

Her pen paused over the page for several seconds. "A good *breeder?" Oh goodness. I get all kinds in here!*

"Yes. Wide hips, sturdy pelvis, that sort of thing."

"Hmm, oookaaay." The scribbling continued. "How about looks?"

"Nice looking, but I don't want a woman who attracts too much attention from other men." His eyes narrowed in painful remembrance of the last great beauty he'd allowed too close. "I don't share."

She scribbled something on the page before her. "So, let's say average beauty. And educational level?"

"Smart enough to know not to betray me." Derrick crossed his ankle over his knee to pick off a piece of lint that had gotten trapped in the cuff of his perfectly creased pant leg.

"Hmm…" Her thin brows crinkled as she continued to scribble. "And personality?"

"Good with kids, not too demanding of my time, and financially self-sufficient." He snorted. "If I wanted to take care of something, I'd adopt a puppy."

Derrick watched uneasily as she laid the pen down, slowly closed the manila file, and folded her hands together on top of it.

"Mr. Brandt, I was under the impression you were looking for a permanent relationship, a wife."

"I am."

"Then, I must say, I'm a little surprised by your responses so far." She reopened the file and glanced down at what she'd written. "An average-looking woman, who will apparently spend her life in fear of your wrath and be at your beck and call. Not to mention that she is expected to fully support herself despite your wealth and resources." She glanced at him. "I have to admit, I can't think of a single woman in my client profiles who fits such a description."

"Well, I guess you are going to have to expand your client-profile list."

She shut the file once more, and sat back in the chair. "Or…you're going to have to find another matchmaker."

Derrick flinched inwardly, knowing he was about to blow an interview that meant much more to him than he could ever let on. He nervously picked at his pant leg as his mind calculated the best way forward.

On some level, Derrick understood that despite his financial success, Love Unlimited was probably his best chance at romantic happiness.

For the past ten years, Derrick had dated countless women in the pursuit of one—just one…the *right one*, and had yet to find her.

What he had found instead was his fiancée, Anita, in bed with his college roommate, Chris. He'd also found Carol, the stewardess who had stolen his Amex Black card and taken a group of girlfriends on a one-week, eight-thousand-dollar vacation to Cabo. As pathetic as it was, Derrick knew in his heart that he would've forgiven her for the theft. Eight thousand dollars wasn't even a dent in his wallet. No, it wasn't the theft that had ended the relationship, but the advanced case of crabs she had brought back from the trip.

Then there was Mira, a reporter for the *Philadelphia Herald,* whom he discovered was willing to do just about anything, including sleeping with a man—him— she apparently despised, all for the sake of getting enough inside information for a front-page exposé.

Opening the morning paper to find his pillow talk smeared across the front page was a particularly painful blow. Especially considering the engagement ring he'd purchased for her the day before.

There were others, many other failed relationships with fault lying on both sides to varying degrees. Derrick had almost given up hope of ever finding a compatible woman to spend his life with.

Then, about a month ago, his business partner, Camille, dropped a small article on his desk. It was a lifestyle piece about a small local matchmaking service boasting a one hundred percent compatibility rate among its clientele.

From the moment he walked through the glass double doors of Love Unlimited that morning, Derrick had known there was something special about Noelle Brown. Although, he couldn't fully identify the sensation, he trusted her. And Derrick was a man who took instinct seriously. Most of his present success could be owed to following his gut.

Along with an astute understanding of human nature that had served him well in business if not in his personal relationships, Derrick had overcome incredible odds to become one of the most successful architects in Philadelphia.

Now all he sought to complete his life was the one missing piece of the puzzle, someone trustworthy to share it with. A woman with the social grace and poise of Camille. The emotional openness of a rose in bloom. And the carnal appetite of a nymphomaniac.

Looking at the beauty sitting across from him, Derrick couldn't help wondering about Noelle Brown's carnal appetites. His eyes flashed to the small solitaire diamond wedding ring on her finger. *Lucky Mr. Brown.*

He cleared his throat and sat up straighter. "Why don't you tell me which part of what I've said you find the most difficult to work with."

She gestured to the file. "All of it. But if I had to pick one specific thing, it would be the financial require-ment. I can't think of a single woman who would agree to marry you and then be expected to continue to support herself completely. You're one of the wealthi-est men in Philadelphia, and a marriage is a partnership, Mr. Brandt."

She lifted a knowing eyebrow. "And the *'smart enough not to betray me'* thing. Quite frankly, that state-ment causes me a great deal of alarm."

Hearing it repeated back like that, it did sound bad to Derrick. Eloquence was never his strong suit. He knew that if he ever found the right woman, he would worship her with lavish gifts every day and ravenous at-tention to her body every night. He would hold her as the dearest thing in his life, considering the many years he'd waited for her.

As always, he didn't have the right, diplomatic words often needed to express his feelings when it came to his love life. Instead, his eyes said it all. A problem that had haunted him his whole life and had cost him greatly on more than one occasion.

Camille was always telling Derrick that he had no filter. That something in the brain that kept people from saying exactly what they were thinking seemed to be lacking in him. It always had been. That lack of tact on his part had also contributed to bringing him to this point in his life, where he was requiring professional help in the most basic of human pursuits. The hunt for a mate.

"Maybe I didn't articulate my thoughts properly." He

frowned. "Naturally, I would support my wife, with the usual contingencies. But as for the selection process, let's be perfectly clear. I won't allow you to present me with a handful of money-grubbing, promiscuous opportunists."

For several seconds, Noelle sat staring at him in silence. Derrick stared back.

Finally, she blinked and released a deep sigh. "I will probably regret asking, but feel I must. What exactly do you mean by 'the usual contingencies'?"

"Prenuptial agreements, of course."

"Of course," she muttered, with another deep sigh. She reopened the file and started writing.

Every instinct in Noelle wanted to tell the illustrious Derrick Brandt to get the hell out of her office. The problem was that she could not afford to. She needed him as much as he obviously needed her. Of course, she wasn't about to let him know that.

For a few moments, she'd been terrified that he'd take her up on the offer to find another matchmaker. Thankfully, he'd stayed. Now, the question was…what to do with him?

The man was a Neanderthal, no doubt about it. But he was a wealthy, influential, well-connected Neanderthal. And if handled right, he could be just the boon her growing agency needed.

In the eighteen months since she'd opened her doors, she'd successfully matched almost forty couples. And of that forty, twenty-nine had married, and the other eleven were still together. It was an enviable record by any standard. Despite the lofty name of the agency, Love Unlimited, her resources were indeed *limited* and had been concentrated on rising rent and the day-to-day business of running the agency, leaving little for the kind of advertising and publicity Noelle would've liked. With one positive endorsement, Derrick Brandt could change all that. He could put Love Unlimited over the edge. That is, if she could stomach the man long enough to find a woman willing to put up with him.

She finished her notes and turned the file in his direction. "Okay, I just need you to complete this application and these disclosures." She flipped through the pages. "Sign here and here."

His eyes shot up to meet hers, and she was once again startled by the unusual flickers of gold that surrounded the light green pupils, both colors in stark contrast to those long, lush black lashes. *It's ridiculous for a man to have lashes that long,* she thought.

The unique color was not the most unsettling thing about his eyes. It was the open window to every thought behind them. Whatever Derrick Brandt was thinking or feeling was plainly expressed in those eyes.

"I don't sign anything without reading it first." He sat back once again crossed his ankle over his knee and settled in to read the file. Derrick smoothed his silk tie, reached inside his jacket pocket and pulled out a pen. Using it as a guide, he began reading. Noelle frowned at his downcast head, still unsure just what to make of him.

Granted, he was probably the most beautiful specimen of masculinity she'd ever laid eyes on. Granted, he was rich as King Solomon and showed flashes of intelligence that bordered on brilliant. But even with all that going for him, it was hard to like the man. It had all started with that smile. Noelle felt her blood beginning to boil once more just remembering.

* * *

Her secretary, Terri, had called in sick because her daughter had come down with the flu. Noelle understood the woes of a sick child, but it had created a problem, considering she had five appointments scheduled for the day, the first and most important of which was going to arrive any minute.

She had been scrambling around on Terri's desk, looking for the phone number of the temporary agency she occasionally used, when the glass doors to her suite were thrown open, and he walked in. Derrick Brandt.

Noelle immediately recognized him. His face was in the paper almost every week. The photographic images did not do him justice. He stood, tall and broad shouldered, and moved with the precision of a dancer. His handsome face look chiseled from stone, all sharp angles and perfect lines. His light-colored almond-shaped eyes were in startling contrast to his rich brown skin. A sharp nose and heart-shaped pink lips completed the exquisite picture. Looking at Derrick Brandt, one would never guess he had gotten his start in life as a mailroom clerk for a Philadelphia architectural firm. A firm he now owned.

As he entered, Noelle stood straight and walked around the desk with her hand extended in greeting, fully prepared to be her professional best. As her eyes met his, she stopped in her tracks with several feet still between them.

His hazel-green eyes twinkled with wolfish delight as he openly, blatantly and completely without shame ogled her! There was no other word for it.

Noelle stood stunned. No man had ever looked at her like that before. At least not that *she* had seen. She had to fight the compulsion to cover herself with her hands as he mentally stripped her of every article of clothing.

Then, as if that scathing examination were not insulting enough, he looked her directly in the eyes, and *he smiled.* Not just any smile. No, this smile held sinister promise.

Watching the ravenous expression fade from his eyes when they fell to her left hand, Noelle was very grateful for the diamond wedding ring she wore as a prop. She'd originally bought it to lend credibility to her role as a matchmaker. Most people understandably wanted to believe that their matchmaker was herself a happily married woman. *Maybe one day but* not *anytime soon.*

Determined to ignore his lascivious behavior, she pasted on her best smile and continued moving forward with her hand extended in greeting. "Welcome to Love Unlimited, Mr. Brandt. Noelle Brown."

He frowned. "You're Noelle Brown?"

Didn't I just say that? She ground her teeth together, determined to keep the false smile firmly in place. "Yes, I am. It's so nice to meet you," she lied.

Gesturing behind her, she said, "Please come into my office. Would you like a cup of coffee or tea?"

"Neither," he grumbled.

She turned and walked back into her office. "A bottle of water, perhaps?"

"That will be fine. Thank you."

Noelle crossed behind the desk, opened the small fridge built into her credenza and pulled out two bottles of water. Reaching across the desk, she placed one in front of the guest chair.

As Noelle took her seat, she tried very hard to wipe the memory of that smile from her mind, determined to make the best of this golden opportunity. But as she watched the porn movie playing in his mind reflected in his eyes, it proved impossible.

She'd only known him five minutes, and she could already see the signs of why this man, who was said to have the magical touch of King Midas in his business dealings, was such a blazing failure at romantic relationships.

She'd just met the man and already didn't like him. She could only imagine what other women must think. *You don't have to like him. Just tolerate him,* Noelle reminded herself. He was the key to Love Unlimited's future success. Finding Derrick Brandt a mate would put her small matchmaking agency on the map. Permanently.

For years, Noelle had read the stories in all the local papers regarding Derrick Brandt's professional successes and personal flops. Usually businessmen did not garner the kind of media coverage Derrick received. With his rags-to-riches background and camera-perfect face, he was a fascinating figure to the citizens of Philadelphia. Especially when it became obvious that, despite his financial acumen, he had the social grace of a camel. As far as the local tabloids were concerned, Derrick Brandt was the best kind of celebrity figure: prone to public emotional outbursts.

He argued with his girlfriends in busy restaurants. He assaulted cameramen who got too close. He had a well-known reputation for being rude and surly, the by-product of which was that for the right price, people in the service industry were eager to betray him. He was considered a playboy, although not a very successful one.

In other words, Derrick Brandt was a paparazzi dream come true. The local media had even gone so far as to give him the odious label of *The Most Ineligible Bachelor in the City.*

And now the man—and all the media attention that went along with him—was sitting in Noelle's office seeking her help in finding his perfect mate. When he'd called her last week to schedule the appointment, Noelle had immediately seen the opportunity for what it was. The chance of a lifetime.

Finding the right woman for Derrick Brandt would garner media attention for her firm that could not be bought. It would be said that *if Love Unlimited could find a match for the most ineligible bachelor in Philadelphia, they could find a match for anyone!* Noelle could already see the headlines, and the droves of new clients that would follow.

First, in order to do that, she would have to put her personal dislike for the lecherous man aside and apply herself to doing what she did best. Matching couples based on common interest, physical attraction and the most likely long-term compatibility. Or, in Derrick Brandt's case...finding *Ms. Right* for *Mr. Wrong.*

Chapter 2

The light tapping on the door alerted Derrick to the identity of his visitor even before the door opened. A gray head of hair peeked around the edge, and Derrick could not resist the smile that came to his lips whenever she walked into the room. Camille Massey, his business partner, his benefactor, his friend…his savior.

The elderly woman started to enter the room until she realized Derrick was on the phone. She started to back out, but he raised a hand to halt her.

"I have another meeting to get to. Can we wrap this up?" He spoke into the intercom while motioning Camille to come in.

He listened to some final comments, but his attention was riveted on Camille as she made her way across the room. She was moving more slowly than usual today. He frowned, knowing what that meant: her rheumatism was acting up again. Derrick was tempted to drop the phone and go help her. But Camille was a proud woman who would not welcome his assistance. The meeting was called to an end. Derrick said his good-byes and hung up the phone.

He sat back in his plush leather chair, waiting while she settled into the guest chair at the side of his desk, a large, comfortable wingback chair he kept there just for her, knowing the small if stylish guest chairs that decorated the rest of the office suite were uncomfortable to her brittle bones.

"Why aren't you using one of the walking canes I bought you?" he asked gruffly, watching as she straightened the pleats of her skirt around her.

"Because I don't need them," she muttered and, once satisfied with her appearance, settled back in the chair. "Well?"

Derrick knew exactly what she was waiting for, but he wasn't about to make it easy. "Well?"

Her soft brown eyes narrowed menacingly. "Don't play with me, boy."

Derrick burst into laughter. "Why not? You play with everyone else. We're all just puppets on your strings, myself included."

"Am I going to have to call over there myself?"

"You wouldn't."

She smirked. "Has twenty-five years with me taught you nothing?"

Derrick sat up in the chair. "Okay, you would. But don't."

"Then answer me."

He sighed in defeat. "It went fine."

"Fine? That's all? Did they find a lady friend for you?"

"Camille, it's not a supermarket. You don't walk in and grab a girl off the shelf and carry her to the checkout lane. These things take time."

She frowned. "How much time? You don't wear well."

He frowned back. "More than one day, that's for sure. Apparently, she had to—"

"Who's she?"

"Noelle Brown, the owner."

Camille stared into his eyes for several seconds before her face spread into a wide grin. "Well, well… Tell me about this Ms. Brown."

"Before you start cackling in glee, that's *Mrs.* Brown."

The smile disappeared. "Married? Humph, that's too bad. I haven't seen that look in your eyes at the mention of a woman in years."

"Yeah, well, it won't be that woman. You know how I feel about sharing."

"Unfortunately," she muttered, toying with the pleats of her skirt, "half of Philadelphia knows how you feel about sharing."

Derrick decided to let the comment slide instead of getting into another argument about his lack of discretion last year, when he heard his then-girlfriend, Mira, was out club-hopping with another man. The media had made sure Derrick was aware of the situation and then sat back with their cameras ready and let Derrick be…Derrick.

Looking back, he would be the first to admit he did not handle it well, but controlling his emotions had never been easy. All he could remember was the pure rage he felt walking into the nightclub and seeing his woman pressed against another man on the dance floor. Later, Derrick would discover the man was Mira's old college friend Byron, who also happened to be a happily committed gay man. By the time he discovered these facts, it would be too late to straighten things out with Mira. Because soon after, she would betray him on the front page of the *Herald* with the revealing exposé titled "The Man Behind The Myth."

"Mira wasn't the one anyway," he muttered, feeling some need to defend his actions.

Camille twisted her mouth in a silent expression that spoke volumes.

"Did you see the plans for the Marquardt Building?" he asked, seeking to end the discussion regarding his troubled love life.

"Yes. When are you presenting them?"

"Next week." He watched as she rubbed her right knee. "Are you okay?"

She smiled sadly. "Yes, just the cost of living too long."

Derrick looked into the wise old eyes of the woman who'd come to mean so much to him and once again wondered where he would've ended up had it not been for the intervention of Camille Massey.

"Where would I have ended up if you hadn't intervened in my life?"

Camille snorted. "You would've been just fine. You're tough as nails, Derrick Brandt. You always have been."

He huffed. "Who are you kidding? We both know I was a statistic just waiting to happen." His eyes took on a faraway look as he remembered his troubled childhood. "If you hadn't given me a job that day I showed up here." He shook his head.

"Well, I did." She rubbed her knee once more before struggling to her feet. Derrick was instantly at her elbow, gently steadying her. "And I have never regretted the decision." She looked directly into his eyes, and Derrick couldn't help feeling a sense of pride. She'd believed in him, and he'd gone out of his way to make sure she never stopped.

"Just keep me up to date on how things are progressing," she said, heading to the door.

"All right, but not much should change between now and when we present the plans next week—"

She stopped and made a dismissive gesture with her hand. "Boy, I don't care about the Marquardt Building! I'm sure you've got that completely under control. It's your personal life that's a mess."

Derrick leaned against his desk and folded his arms across his chest. "Why this sudden interest in my love life?"

Derrick watched the brief sadness cross her face, but she quickly covered it with a smile. "Somebody needs to start taking a vested interest in it." She started walking again. "Lord knows we can't depend on your judgment."

As Derrick watched her leave the room, he wondered if Camille had any idea just how close to the truth she really was.

Chapter 3

Together the couple leaned forward and gustily blew out the forty white candles on the beautifully decorated cake.

"Happy anniversary!" The room erupted in applause and well wishes for the happy couple standing at the head of the long, formal dining table.

As Kimber, Noelle's older sister, stepped forward with a cake knife to begin dividing up the dessert, the crowd of family and friends gathered closer to offer hugs and congratulations to Gilbert and Claudia Brown. They were celebrating their fortieth wedding anniversary.

Noelle could not hide the wistful expression on her face as she watched her parents gaze at each other as if they were the only two people in the world. They had always looked at each other like that, and Noelle knew they always would.

She felt a tug on her pant leg. "Auntie."

Noelle glanced down at her niece Lea, who was trying to get her attention.

The toddler grabbed the crotch of her pants. "Pee-pee, Auntie, pee-pee."

Noelle quickly scanned the room and found her sister-in-law, Ann, standing with a group of family friends on the other side of the large dining room. Swooping the two-year-old up in her arms, Noelle quickly maneuvered her way through the crowd in her parents' house.

"Hurry, Auntie, got go bad," Lea whined, then promptly stuck the two middle fingers of her right hand in her mouth and began to suck on them like a pacifier.

Noelle quickened her pace. She knew from experience that once the finger sucking began, the clock was ticking. She elbowed and excused her way out of the crowded room and took the stairs to the second level, down the hall to the bathroom.

Once inside, she quickly slid Lea's elastic waist pants down her short legs, along with the Huggies training diaper, and plopped the little girl on the toilet seat and waited.

After a moment, there was a small tinkling noise and then nothing.

Lea's eyes lit up. "Auntie! Good girl!"

Noelle felt her heart swell with love and pride. "Yes, sweetheart, you are such a good girl." She helped Lea re-dress and then hugged her close. "Look what you did. You're becoming a big girl."

Noelle lifted the small body up to the sink for hand washing, which was Lea's favorite part of the process. She smeared soap on her hands over and over, playing in the water.

Just as Noelle exited, her brother, Raymond, came

charging over into the bathroom carrying a little girl who was an exact replica of Lea.

When Ray and Noelle's eyes met, the pair burst into laughter.

"Lena, too?" Noelle said, but Ray was too busy trying to get his second twin daughter settled on the toilet seat to stop for conversation.

Unlike Lea, Lena's bladder was completely full and took several seconds to empty. While they waited, Ray leaned back against the door and closed his eyes.

The sounds of laughter, the occasional clinking of their mother's fine china and the mellow sounds of the music of John Legend created a cacophony of sound drifting up to Noelle and Ray from the party below.

"You look tired." Noelle noted the dark rings under her brother's eyes and realized it was the first time she'd seen him in almost a week, which was unusual for her tight-knit family.

Ray smiled at his little sister. "Good to see you, too."

"I don't mean you look bad." She playfully bumped up against him. "Just tired. Are you just now getting here? I didn't see you earlier."

He yawned sleepily. "Yeah, just finished a seventy-two-hour rotation at the hospital." He reached down to help Lena, who was climbing down from the toilet seat.

"Look, Daddy!" Lena pulled up her Huggies diaper and pants before turning to point to the contents of the toilet.

Ray gave his sister a slight grimace before forcing himself to look into the toilet. "Wonderful, baby girl. You did wonderful."

Not about to let her sister steal her thunder, Lea pushed her way between them. "Part of that me!" she declared, frowning up at her father.

"Well, you both did terrific. My little ladies are growing up." He ran his large hand over the top of their matching curly afro puffs. Satisfied with the praise, the girls raced out of the bathroom.

"Hey, wait, Lena, you didn't wash your hands!" Noelle made a grab for her, but they were already halfway down the stairs.

"Remind me not to eat anything Lena offers," Ray chuckled as he reached forward to flush the toilet.

Noelle watched him silently. Every line in his body expressed sheer exhaustion. "The woes of being an ER doctor?"

Ray glanced up at her. "No." He shook his head. "Trust me, little sis, the long hours—that's the easy part of the job."

Noelle understood at once. Unfortunately, she'd seen that sadness in her brother's eyes before. Ray had lost a patient that day. "Wanna talk about it?"

He smiled softly. "No, but thanks for asking." He crowded beside her at the sink to wash his hands. "So, what did you give Mom and Dad for their anniversary?"

"What do I always give them?"

"Not another gift certificate for dinner. For someone who makes her living creating romance, you sure stink at romantic milestone gifts."

"By the time I finish making romance for my clients, I have no inspiration left for myself," Noelle joked but instantly regretted it when her brother's eyes sharpened on her face.

"You know, I've often thought that about you."

Noelle could see where the conversation was going. Another one of her sibling's infamous and indiscreet inquiries into her nonexistent social life.

In an attempt to steer it away from that direction, she folded her arms across her chest and glared at her brother. "Okay, Mr. Romance, what did you get them?"

"An all-expense-paid weekend at a romantic spa retreat in the Poconos."

"Uh-huh." Noelle frowned in disbelief. "That had to be Ann's idea."

"So what?" Ray didn't even bother to deny that his wife was the brains behind it. "I still get credit for it."

"Cheater."

"Sticks and stones, Cupid, sticks and stones. So how's the matchmaking business?"

Noelle hesitated sharing her good news for only a moment. "Great, actually. I picked up a very influential client today. If I find him a match, Love Unlimited will finally get some big play in the press. It'll be in the big leagues!"

"Really? Who?"

"Derrick Brandt."

"The architect?"

"One and the same."

"Wow—way to go, kid. That's definitely a name."

Despite his words, something about Ray's tone said he was less than enthused.

"What?"

Ray scratched his chin. "Isn't that guy kinda known for being, well…something of a jackass to his girlfriends?"

Noelle winced. "Not just to his girlfriends. What about it?"

"I was just thinking that if you do find a match for him, great. But what if you don't? I mean, someone in his position could make a lot of trouble for you, make it sound like the fault was with Love Unlimited—not him. Know what I mean?"

"Yeah, unfortunately I do. I hadn't really thought about what would happen if I can't make a match for him. Not to sound arrogant—but I always make the match. The idea of failing never occurred to me. But I admit, after meeting this guy, I am a little worried. He's a total jerk. He spent the whole interview ogling me."

Ray's eyes widened. "Really?"

Noelle's thin brows crinkled in indignation. "No need to sound so shocked, Ray. Men do hit on me from time to time, you know."

"That's not what I meant. He just looks so *GQ*ish. And you…you know."

Noelle found the remarks surprisingly insulting, which was amazing considering some of the insults she and her siblings had exchanged over the years. Instead of letting him off the hook, she kept her silence and waited, watching to see how he would dig his way out of the remark.

"You know! You're…so…Goody Two-shoes."

"Are you kidding me? Goody Two-shoes? Me?"

"Oh, yeah."

Just then, Ann peeked her head around the door. "Ray, when did you arrive? The girls just came downstairs and said Auntie and Daddy were in the bathroom. That sounded kind of strange, so I thought I better check it out. What are you guys doing up here? You're missing the party."

Ray crossed the room to his wife without delay. "Hi, honey. How was your day?" He mimicked his wife's high-pitched voice.

Ann smirked. "Hi, honey." She stepped up on her tiptoes to kiss his cheek. "How was your day?"

Wrapping her in a tight embrace, he sighed into her hair. "Better, now that I'm with you."

The sincerity in his voice melted Noelle's heart, and she suddenly had the feeling of being an intruder. *This is what it's all about,* Noelle thought. Ray and Ann, her parents—they were the couples that had inspired her to start Love Unlimited.

Despite the nickname of Cupid bestowed on her by her brother, Noelle had never believed that there was necessarily one soul mate for any one person. She thought it more likely that there were certain people who just fit together better than others. And that if given the proper tools and assistance, those people could find each other rather than spending their lives going from one bad fit to the next. Because when it was right, there was a kind of magic that happened. Like what she was witnessing now.

With their arms wrapped around each other, the couple turned to leave.

"Ray, what did you mean by that Goody Two-shoes remark?" Noelle hated to interrupt, given the day Ray had obviously had. She knew all he wanted was some time with his wife. But the comment was bugging her, and she couldn't seem to let it go.

"Nothing—I meant nothing by it." With his arm still around his wife's small waist, Ray turned back to face his sister. "Noelle. You are a beautiful, intelligent, successful woman, and you deserve only the best. But if even half of what I've heard about that guy is true, he's bad news. Just…keep it professional."

As the couple neared the stairs, Noelle heard Ann ask Ray, "What guy?" Their voices faded down the stairs before Noelle heard his reply.

Noelle leaned against the shower door and considered her brother's words. She couldn't shake the feeling that, whether intentionally or not, Ray had expressed more than he'd meant to. In fact, he'd probably expressed the same feelings anyone would upon hearing that superfine Derrick Brandt had come on to her: amazement.

Noelle had no delusions about her physical appearonce. She was of average looks, nothing stunning, but she'd certainly drawn the attention of more than one man in her lifetime. In fact, Noelle was certain that if she were a smaller, more demure woman, she would probably be considered extremely attractive. But she wasn't a smaller, demure woman. Standing barefoot at almost five-ten, she felt like a giant. And not even an elegant giant, like the regal models the world admired. She was plump.

Of course, the people who loved her called her big boned, but Noelle knew the difference. Her bones were not the problem. It was the meat on the bones, and there was more of it than she'd like. The result of a lifelong sweet tooth and overindulgent parents.

Noelle, and her siblings, Kimber and Ray, had each inherited their father's build. Of course, on Ray it was considered an attractive feature. What woman didn't love a big, strapping man to wrap her arms around? Ann certainly seemed to appreciate his height and girth. And even Kimber, although tall, had done a better job of resisting the after-dinner desserts of their childhood, and instead of being *big boned,* she'd turned out long and willowy. Men loved long, willowy women.

No, Noelle knew she was the only one of her siblings for whom the inheritance of their father's genetics had not been a plus. At home, it had not in any way been a hindrance. She'd grown up in a house full of love and had never been given the feeling of being anything less than fantastic.

Gilbert and Claudia Brown had managed to do what all the daytime talk shows thought impossible. They'd managed to raise three emotionally stable, financially successful, well-balanced human beings. And after spending the first five years of her professional adult life as a licensed marriage counselor, Noelle had developed a greater appreciation of the uniqueness of her family.

That deeply rooted love, that feeling of complete acceptance, was what had made it so easy for her to give up her career as a counselor and open Love Unlimited.

Although stunned at first by such a drastic move, it hadn't taken her family long to get behind the idea, and now she had their full support. And that of her happily matched clients.

As Noelle started down the stairs, she considered her brother's words once more, and was certain of his meaning. Although he meant no harm, Ray was right. If handled properly, Derrick Brandt could be very good for business. But if not…

Noelle didn't want to dwell on that too long. She had already discovered three women in her database that just might fit the profile for Mr. Brandt. Once she started sending him on dates, he would forget all about his momentary interest in her.

What happened in her office today was just the knee-jerk reaction of a man accustomed to chasing anything in a skirt. Noelle had seen the kinds of women Derrick Brandt chose to date in scores of pictures she pulled off the Internet while preparing for their interview.

But she knew Derrick Brandt's type, and she *definitely* was not it.

As much of a brute as he was, he was just so *sexy*. A real walk-through-fire-for-his-woman type of man.

Chapter 4

Noelle Brown was *exactly* his type. Derrick couldn't seem to stop thinking about the woman. Even as he sat at the head of the long conference table, only partially listening to the conversations going on around him.

At the last minute, he'd discovered a glitch in the plan for the Marquardt Building. The engineering firm wanted their building to be the preeminent example of new-age design. They wanted their building to say something. A symbol of stability to their clients and an intimidating foe to their competitors. The board of directors for Marquardt had a bold and daring vision for their new building.

Unfortunately, their vision did not include the ten emergency exits that were required by state code. And now, Derrick and his team of thirty had to find a way to include the necessary exits without diminishing the overall appeal of the building. This was a potentially disastrous development in this crucially important project, and yet…Derrick couldn't care less.

All he wanted to do was go back to his office and call Love Unlimited. He just wanted to hear her voice. He knew he had a valid excuse. He could say he was calling for an update. It had been a full week since he'd interviewed with Noelle Brown, and she hadn't so much as dropped him an e-mail regarding the status of his case. For the first two days, Derrick had been in a panic, taking her complete silence as a bad sign. He'd wondered if she'd reconsidered taking him on as a client after he'd left the office and had decided against finding the match. After the third day, his nerves had settled. That was when his accountant had informed him that the check he'd written as a deposit for her services had cleared the bank. So now, regrets or no, Noelle Brown was stuck with him.

He wondered what she was wearing at that very moment. Maybe another one of those form-fitting silk blouses that gave a little but not too much. He closed his eyes and tried to once again conjure the smell of her unusual perfume.

"What do you think, Derrick?" He recognized the voice of Tom, one of his chief engineers. The thin white man was standing beside Derrick's chair.

What the hell am I doing? She's a married woman. Derrick blinked and quickly replayed the last thing he'd heard. When he told Noelle Brown that he did not share his women, he meant it. No matter how desirable that woman was.

"Derrick?"

"Yeah, it might work. But the fire-resistant standard

metal doors that we use for emergency exits won't fit that scheme," he answered smoothly.

"What if we paint them?" one of his interns nervously offered from the other end of the table.

"Paint them?" Tom whined. "What the hell difference would that make?"

Derrick stood and touched Tom on the shoulder to still the tongue-lashing he knew was about to be unleashed on the poor, unsuspecting man.

"That's one suggestion. What's your name again?" Derrick asked. There were always so many of them coming and going, it was hard to keep track.

The young man's eyes widened when he realized who was addressing him. "K-K-Kenneth Pike, sir."

Derrick smiled. "Can I call you Kenny?"

Kenny grinned widely. "Yes, sir."

"Derrick," Tom interrupted, "painting the damn doors is not going to—"

Derrick put up his hand to silence Tom. "Kenny, Tom here is opposed to your idea of painting the doors to create an illusion of continuity. On the surface, it sounds feasible, but there is a slight flaw in your suggestion. Can you think of what it might be?"

Everyone waited, allowing Kenny time to discover his own mistake. Several of the architects there had run this gauntlet before. Having their brain pitted against the brain of the master. None revealed the answer, for they knew if Kenny discovered it for himself he would be the better for it. The next time such a discussion occurred, he would think the problem through, instead of just blurting out his first thought.

Derrick watched as Kenny's face crumpled.

"The fire-retardant paint on the doors," Kenny finally

said. "We can't paint over the fire-retardant paint."
Kenny slumped farther down in his chair.

Derrick smiled. "Very good, Kenny." He winked.
"We're going to make an architect out of you eventually." A few chuckles came from around the room.

Kenny hid a shy smile, secretly pleased by the praise.

Tom frowned at Derrick. "Derrick, no one appreciates your snatch-the-pebble-from-my-hand Kung Fu
wisdom more than I, but we have to present completed
plans to the Marquardt board of directors by the end of
the week. So if you don't mind—"

"Kenny, this is not the kind of architect you want to be,
by the way." Derrick poked his thumb toward Tom. A
couple of playful affirmatives came from around the room.

"He's not, sir," Kenny said, with loving eyes for
Derrick alone.

Ignoring Kenny's smitten expression, Derrick walked over to the middle of the table, where the plans were
spread out. Derrick briefly wondered if that was the
look Royce Massey had seen in his eyes when Derrick
was a young intern studying under him.

Of course it was, Derrick decided. No one had a
greater respect and admiration for Royce than the young
thug he'd taken in off the street and trained from the
ground up at the request of his beloved wife. And no one
envied Royce's life more than that young thug. And
now, twenty-five years later, that young thug was living
the life…only not as well.

Despite the incredible wealth he'd accumulated over
the years, despite all the marvelous structures around the
city that were a testament to his great skill as a building
designer, never did Derrick fool himself into believing
he'd lived up to the legacy of Royce Massey. Never

once did Derrick allow himself to believe that he in any way wore the mantle of greatness and dignity that even now enshrouded the memory of his idol.

Taking a quick look at the plans, Derrick made a decision. "Okay, here and here—" he pointed along the drawings "—I want a beam running the length of the frame, slightly overhanging. And then—" he turned the drawings, pulling up the interior blueprint "—we'll put another structural beam here to support it, you see?"

Tom was peering over his shoulder. "Okay, I see what you mean. And the beams would also conceal the exits from the outside of the building."

"Exactly." Derrick nodded. By that time, Kenny along with several others had crept forward to examine the blueprints.

"Everybody got that?" Derrick quickly scanned the group. Once he was satisfied with their understanding, he pushed his way back through the group. "Okay, Tom, take the lead. I've got something I need to take care of. Oh, and Tom, I want Kenny on this project."

Just as he was approaching the conference-room double doors, Derrick heard the voice of Kenny whisper, "He's a lot nicer than I heard."

"Don't believe everything you hear," a female voice whispered back.

As he walked along the plush carpeted hallway leading to his office suite, Derrick wondered just what Kenny had heard. He knew that rumors of his exploits, which were greatly exaggerated, usually made the rounds in the office. He thought he had a reputation of being a fair employer, but now he believed that his personal life was starting to put his work persona in jeopardy.

Not for the first time, Derrick considered just dropping out of the spotlight. Becoming a hermit and hoping that the media would lose interest in him. As quickly as the idea came, it was gone. For reasons he would not consider too closely, Derrick knew that part of him reveled in the attention. For a kid who'd been knocked around the system and basically ignored for most of his youth, the public interest was more than flattering; it was recompense.

He greeted his employees with smiles and the occasional nod as he passed through the open third-floor space that made up the Massey Architectural firm. Instead of going straight into his office, he turned into the adjoining reception area he shared with Camille.

"Morning, Marjorie." He greeted the secretary they shared before glancing at the closed office door next to his. "Is she in?"

Marjorie shook her head. "No, sir. She called this morning and left this message for you." She handed him a folded piece of paper.

Derrick frowned. "Why didn't you give it to me sooner?" Derrick unfolded the note, remembering Camille's slow, painful movements of the previous day.

"She asked me not to until your meeting was over."

Derrick's eyes quickly scanned the note.

Derrick, I won't be in today. Not feeling my best. Camille.

"Get her on the phone." Derrick balled the note and tossed it into the garbage can beside the desk. "And transfer the call to my office."

Before Marjorie could respond, he'd entered his

office and slammed the door shut. Derrick walked across the room and slumped in his waiting chair.

He was worried. He couldn't help it. For Camille to feel bad enough to stay away from the office said a lot. Derrick could only remember her staying home a handful of days in the past year, and, considering her age, that spoke volumes about her strong constitution. Strong willed or not, Camille was still a seventy-year-old woman, and no one was more conscious of that fact than Derrick.

In fact, he probably thought about her mortality more than his own. Camille was the closest thing to family he had, and once she was gone…

His phone rang, and he snatched it from the base. "Yes?"

"I have Mrs. Massey on the line, sir."

"Thank you, Marjorie. Put her through."

After a series of clicks, Derrick heard Camille's disgruntled voice, and it eased his troubled heart.

"You better have a good reason for waking me, young man."

Derrick smiled, feeling more relieved than he could've ever explained. "Just making sure you're still alive."

"I'll admit I'm not long for this world, but I haven't left just yet. Now, why are you on the phone with me instead of in the conference room with your team working out the last-minute kinks in the Marquardt Building plans?"

"That's already squared away. I was just curious as to what could keep the indomitable Camille Massey away from the office."

There was a long pause, and Derrick waited patiently, knowing Camille was searching for the right words. He knew from experience she would tell him as little as possible. He also knew her reasons were equal parts her protective nature and her pride. And Derrick would sift through her explanation for the truth. They'd been together too long and understood each other too well.

"I'm fine, Derrick. Just tired, that's all." She sighed heavily. "I've been thinking about something lately."

"What's that?"

"Retirement."

"Retirement. You?"

"Don't sound so shocked. You knew I had to retire eventually—or did you expect them to just carry me out of my office one day? Besides, it's not like you need me. You haven't needed me in over three years."

"I'll always need you, Camille."

"You're doing a fine job of running the company without any help from anyone. Royce always knew you would be a wonderful architect someday, but I don't think even he imagined you would do as well as you have."

"But—"

"I've given that company my whole life, Derrick. Don't I deserve to keep some small part of it for myself?"

Derrick was speechless. He had no argument for that obvious truth, except his own selfish desire for her companionship. Finally, he answered. "Of course you do."

"It's just an idea. I'm sure I'll feel well enough to come in tomorrow."

"Camille, I…"

"What is it, Derrick?"

"I just wanted to say thank-you—again, for all you've done for me."

"Oh, for goodness' sake, I'm not dying. Lighten up."

"You can make jokes if you want. But we both know the truth. A lot of people wouldn't have helped me."

"What choice did I have?" She laughed. "When you came charging into the ladies' room that day and stopped dead in your tracks when you saw me."

He smiled to himself remembering the unlikely events that brought Camille into his life twenty-five years ago. "I wasn't thinking, just running, I just didn't want to go to that boys' home, and I knew that was the next stop for me. After hitting my latest foster dad over the head with a chair, there weren't a whole lot of options left for a kid like me."

The other end of the line was quiet for so long, Derrick wondered if he'd lost her. "Camille?"

"Hmm, I'm here. I was just thinking. I've often wondered why you didn't ever explain to the social worker why you hit him, Derrick?"

"What was I supposed to say? That waking up in the middle of the night to find a man standing over my bed freaked me out? I didn't realize until it was too late that he was only there to tuck me in." He huffed. "The last time I woke up to find a man over my bed, he wasn't trying to tuck me in, Camille. So, I acted on instinct."

"And you don't think the social worker would've understood that?"

"Please, by that time I'd been in so much trouble, I don't think she would've believed me if I told her I was black."

She chuckled. "Well, it's not like I did anything special. Despite your best effort, she did find you, remember?"

"But so did you," he added quietly, remembering the day Camille showed up in the boys' home to check on him. "You changed the whole path of my life, and no matter how you downplay it, I'll never forget that. And…I'll never be able to repay you."

"Wanna bet? You just get the corrections made on those Marquardt building plans so we can submit them and receive our nice big commission. You'll be a little richer, and I'll be one step closer to retirement. It's a win-win."

Derrick laughed. "You're impossible, you know that?"

"So you tell me."

He sighed in relief, feeling much better now that he'd talked to her and assured himself she was as spunky and contrary as ever.

"All right, I'll see you tomorrow."

Derrick hung up the phone, took a deep breath and sat back in his chair. The winds of change were blowing, and he did not like their direction. But he also knew there was little he could do about it.

From the day he found her, Camille Massey had been the only constant in Derrick's life. And the neglected little boy that still resided in his soul railed against the idea of her not being a part of his everyday existence.

He tapped his fingers on the top of the desk, trying to find a way to distract himself from his troubling thoughts. He considered all the projects spread on the small mahogany conference table on the other side of his office.

There were also a couple of job sites he'd been putting off visiting. That wasn't what he wanted right now. No, Derrick knew himself well enough to know beyond a shadow of a doubt that when he was feeling this particular brand of melancholy blue, there was only one thing that could lift his spirits. He needed a woman's warmth.

Unfortunately, he was not currently in a relationship nor was he the type of man to dip his wick in any available sweet pot, contrary to the tabloid stories. No, Derrick knew he was a one-woman man. The problem was, he could never seem to find the right woman...

He pulled his wallet from his back pocket and pulled out the elegantly embossed business card. He quickly dialed the number.

"Love Unlimited, Terri speaking."

"Noelle Brown, please."

"I'm sorry, Mrs. Brown is in with a client. Can I help you?"

"When will she be free?"

"May I ask who's calling?"

"Derrick Brandt."

"One moment, Mr. Brandt." She quickly returned to the line. "Mrs. Brown asked that I take a message."

"A message?" *Where the hell are the women you promised me? How's that for a message?*

"Sir?"

"Just ask her to call me. I haven't heard from her in a week, and I'm getting impatient."

"I'll give her the message. Is there anything else I can do for you today?"

Yes, you can tell me what your boss is wearing. Is it silk and clinging to her voluptuous bust? Does she still smell like paradise in a bottle? Is she happily married or just married?

"No, that's all."

"I'll be sure to give her your message. You have a nice day, Mr. Brandt."

Derrick hung up the phone and sat back in his chair. "She's married. She's married. She's married," he chanted to himself.

Determined to get his mind off Noelle Brown, or

any other woman for that matter, he glanced at his work-table once more.

A few minutes later, he was on his feet and headed to the door. As he passed Marjorie, he called over his shoulder, "I'll be out of the office the rest of the day."

Chapter 5

Elegantly dressed and regal in every way, Dr. Suzanne Chambers sat across from Noelle and twisted her nose in disdain. With a shake of her thick, black tresses, she tossed the file on the desk.

"This is *not* a very impressive questionnaire, Noelle. Some of his answers border on rude. What makes you think I would be interested in this guy?"

"Well, granted, he's a little rough around the edges, but with the right woman I think he has a lot of potential."

"Hmm…such as?"

Noelle knew Suzanne was quickly losing what little interest she had shown in the case file of Client 047. "For starters, he's career driven and extremely ambitious." Noelle winked at the woman, who was not only a client but a friend. "Sound like anyone you know?"

Suzanne's mouth twisted in a smirk. "Go on."

"And let's just say I have a feeling that the chemistry would work. Trust me. Just meet him first and then make your decision. I have a feeling about this."

She sighed. "It's just I thought there would be more obvious signs of compatibility. This feels like just another blind date, and heaven knows I've suffered through enough of those for one lifetime."

Noelle hid the sympathy she felt swell up in her heart. She knew exactly what Suzanne was feeling. The two women had much in common, including their physical build. It was one of the things that had factored into Noelle's decision to consider Suzanne as a possible match for Derrick Brandt. Noelle knew that Derrick Brandt, unlike some men, would have no problem with Suzanne's few extra pounds.

"Well, just keep in mind, this blind date is being set up by a professional matchmaker."

Suzanne reached over and picked up the file once more. "I just don't know." Her soft brown eyes focused on Noelle's face. "I'm tired of having my heart broken by guys only interested in my money. I'm ready for something real, Noelle. That's why I came to you."

Noelle reached across the desk and laid her hand over the hand of her client and friend. "Trust me, Suzanne. I think you want to give this guy a chance."

"Well, if you really think—"

"You can't go in there!"

Noelle heard the voice of her assistant rise in alarm.

"I'm tired of waiting. I want to see her now!" an irate male voice responded angrily.

Oh, no. Noelle stood from her desk chair.

"What's that about?" Suzanne turned toward the door with a worried expression.

"Mr. Brandt! You can't—"

Noelle was halfway around the desk when her office door was thrown open.

Derrick Brandt stopped in the middle of the floor as if surprised to see that Terri had indeed been telling him the truth.

"Mr. Brandt, she's with a client!" Terri was charging in the man's wake, and he stopped so abruptly she ran smack into the back of him. Jolted by the impact, she stumbled back, and with lightning reflexes, Derrick turned and caught her before she slipped.

Still fuming in anger, Terri jerked from him without so much as a thank-you and hurried over to the desk. "I'm sorry, Noelle. I tried to stop him, but he wouldn't listen."

"It's okay, Terri."

With one final glare at Derrick, Terri walked back out of the door, gently closing it behind her.

Noelle ran a hand over her forehead, feeling the onset of a migraine. "Mr. Brandt, as you can see, I am in a meeting." She gestured to Suzanne, who sat staring up at Derrick like he was a comet that had just dropped from the sky. "Suzanne Chambers, this is—"

"Derrick Brandt." Suzanne's eyes widened.

Noelle sighed. "Or as you know him, Client 047. Mr. Brandt, I was just discussing your profile with Ms. Chambers." Noelle winced inwardly as Suzanne rose from the chair, stepped forward and extended her hand in greeting…only to have Derrick completely ignore it and walk around her.

"Why haven't you called me all week?" He stopped directly in front of Noelle and stood glaring at her.

"As I was saying, Mr. Brandt, I have been actively working to find a candidate for you, and she's standing right over there."

Derrick glanced over his shoulder at the confused woman. "No. I know her type. It's all about her and her career, and I'm not prepared to be a *Mr.* Chambers."

Stunned by the unprovoked attack, Suzanne charged forward. "How dare you!"

Not knowing what Suzanne planned to do when she reached him, Noelle jumped between the two. "Suzanne, let me deal with him. I'll call you later."

"Fine." She quickly collected her purse and jacket. "But you can scratch my name off the list of potential candidates. I wouldn't date him if you paid me." She stomped toward the door, and then just as quickly turned and stomped back to where Noelle was still standing protectively in front of her client.

"You know, I would've been willing to ignore all the negative things I've read about you and given you the benefit of the doubt. But you just proved yourself to be a bigger ass than the press could've ever." She glanced at Noelle. "Good luck finding a woman willing to accept this jerk." With that she turned and stormed out of the room, slamming the door behind her.

Noelle was fuming with anger at how he'd dismissed the best possible candidate she could find and had so callously insulted her friend.

She took a deep breath—not that it did any good—and swung around to face him. "I hope you're satisfied!"

Derrick was staring down at her left hand. "Where's your ring?"

"Do you realize what you just did? You just chased away the very best chance you had at a compatible match."

The wolfish grin appeared for a brief moment. "Maybe—maybe not. Answer the question."

Suddenly Noelle remembered that she'd taken the

prop ring off the evening before when she'd gone to her parents' anniversary party and had forgotten to put it back on that morning. And from the look in his eyes, Mr. Brandt was becoming suspicious.

Noelle walked around to her seat, putting the desk between them. "Mr. Brandt, I understand you're anxious—"

"Are you married?"

Damn. "Mr. Brandt—"

"It's Derrick." He followed her around the desk. "And answer the question."

The man really is an ass. "That's none of your business." She backed up as much as possible and felt the seat of her chair come up against the back of her legs.

His face spread into the most beautiful smile she'd ever seen as he gently lifted her hand to his lips. "You're not married."

Noelle was unable to speak as she felt his soft, warm lips graze the back of her hand. "What—what are you doing?" She shook off the hypnotic spell he was quickly casting over her, snatching her hand away.

"Are you even engaged?" That beautiful smile was still perfectly in place, showing two rows of white, well-cared-for teeth as his light green eyes bored into her brown ones. "No," he finally pronounced. "You're as single as I am."

Pushing her chair back out of the way, Noelle backed up and took a stand. "Just who do you think you are? Barging in here—interrupting my meeting and demanding personal information. I can't do business this way, Mr. Brandt. It's inconceivable at this point how Love Unlimited could be of benefit to you. Please leave. I will refund your deposit tomorrow. Good-bye."

He turned and walked back around the desk. But instead of leaving, he unbuttoned his suit jacket and took the seat recently vacated by Suzanne. "You know, I realized something was wrong the last time I was here, but I couldn't quite put my finger on it." He gestured to her desktop. "No pictures. You have pictures of family. That one with the couple and the little girls, and the older couple that I would assume are your parents. But no husband, no children of your own."

"Get out!"

The smile fell from his face. "Be careful, Noelle. I understand you're upset, but you might as well settle down. I'm not going anywhere. Especially not now."

Noelle was fuming with rage. If she were able, she would've physically thrown him out of the office. "Who the hell do you think you are?"

With a sigh, he reached into the breast pocket of his suit jacket, pulled out a folded piece of paper and slid it across the desktop.

Despite her pounding head and racing pulse, Noelle was extremely curious as to what was on the paper but was not about to give him the satisfaction of picking it up. "What's that?"

"A financial synopsis of Love Unlimited."

"What?" She quickly grabbed up the paper and scanned the information it contained. "How did you get this?!"

"That's not nearly as important as what it says."

Noelle felt like her legs had been cut out from under her. She blindly reached for her chair and pulled it to her, suddenly nauseated. This man had somehow discovered a truth about her company that even her family did not know.

There in three succint paragraphs was the truth of her

failing business. Despite the success in matching couples, Love Unlimited was going under. Rising rent, overhead, advertising and social events were just so expensive! She was spending faster than she was earning. And though she could've asked her family for a loan, her pride wouldn't allow it.

As if a bucket of freezing water had been poured over her head, Noelle felt herself go from flaming hot anger to icy cold fear. "What are you planning to do with this?" she asked, working to keep her voice from cracking.

The devil across the desk arched an eyebrow. "Nothing. Now we move forward on an even playing field. No more talk of dumping me as a client, and no more barging into your office. Agreed?"

Noelle considered the options. "And…if I don't agree?"

"You lose your best and only chance to pull your company out of the red. Face it, Noelle. You need me as much as I need you." Suddenly he sat forward, and something in his body language conveyed to Noelle a new energy level. Apparently, Lucifer was most energized when bartering for souls. "And I do need you, Noelle.

"I didn't go looking for that information to embarrass you. It surfaced as part of a routine financial check I run on anyone I chose to do business with." His light eyes honed in on her face. "You just witnessed a problem I have been dealing with my entire adult life.

"I…" He shrugged, obviously looking for the right words, and Noelle caught a glimpse of vulnerability. "I'm not good talking to women. I'm blunt and gruff. I'm not ignorant of my problems, but I've had some bad experiences that have left me with little tolerance for bull. I need someone with your expertise."

Unable to just drop the not-so-subtle threat lying on the desk between them, Noelle's eyes narrowed. "So you come in here to blackmail me?"

A quick grin flashed across his face. "Actually, I just picked that up from my attorney on the way over here and had no intention of showing it to you until it became obvious it was the only way to get you to listen to me."

She sat back in her chair and folded her arms across her chest. "So, what now?"

"That's up to you. I hope we can put this behind us and continue to work together."

After several seconds, Noelle let out a long breath. "You can't just barge in here anytime you want."

"I understand that. I thought you were ignoring me."

"Well, I wasn't."

"I realize that now. I apologize."

Several long, tense seconds passed in silence while she considered her options. *What options?* With one little piece of paper, he'd removed any options. And he was right; they did need each other. But could they work together?

"Okay." She snorted. "Although Suzanne was the best candidate I had."

"She's a beautiful woman, and I'm sure a fine person—but she's not for me. I have the utmost faith that you will find someone suitable for me." He stood and buttoned his jacket. "I look forward to hearing from you." With that he walked out of the office.

As soon as the door closed behind him, Noelle grabbed the synopsis off the desk and quickly ran it through the shredder.

* * *

She's not married. Derrick couldn't hide the curve of his lips as he considered the implications of what that meant. *She's not married.*

The elevator reached the bottom floor, and the steel doors opened. He waited patiently for the people surrounding him to exit before moving forward.

As he headed to the rotating glass doors that led to the outside world, he noticed a bright red flower cart sitting off to one side of the marble corridor. As a thought occurred to him, he changed his direction and headed toward the cart.

Ten minutes later, with a spring in his step, Derrick emerged onto the bustling avenue where his driver, Don, waited with his black Lexus. Derrick slipped into the backseat of the car and, giving Don their next destination, settled back with a wide grin on his face.

Chapter 6

One week later, Noelle sat staring at the bouquet of wilting flowers sitting on the corner of her desk, just as she had done every day since they'd arrived unexpectedly. She still had no idea what it meant. Had Mr. Brandt sent the flowers as a truce? Given the way their last meeting ended, that was not an unreasonable assumption. But what if it meant something else?

Noelle could still see the look of triumph that flashed in his eyes when he realized—with certainty—that she was not married. Why was he so certain? She wondered.

She'd never confirmed or denied the claim, yet that something in his eyes left absolutely no doubt as to what he believed. Well, it didn't matter. Either way, the sooner she was rid of Derrick Brandt the better. And it all started this evening with the first of what she hoped were viable candidates.

"Come in."

Terri came into the room and gently pushed the door closed behind her. Leaning back against it, she folded her arms across her chest and glared across the room at Noelle. "It's the jerk. Do you want me to throw him out?"

Noelle suppressed a smile. Derrick Brandt may not have realized it, but he'd made a formidable enemy in Terri. "Don't you dare—not if you want a paycheck at the end of the week."

Terri's mouth twisted into an unwilling smile. "I didn't say I wouldn't take his wallet *before* I threw him out."

"Like it or not, he's our client. So show him in."

Terri huffed. "If you insist. But I think you're fighting a losing battle. The only woman that would be a match for this guy is the bride of Frankenstein." She turned to open the door and paused. "On second thought, dating Derrick Brandt would be lowering her standards." She opened the door wide. "Mr. Brandt, Mrs. Brown can see you now."

Derrick Brandt appeared in the doorway, his light eyes boring into Terri. "By the way, you may want to make sure the door is firmly closed the next time you decide to slander a client."

With a look that conveyed not a single ounce of remorse, Terri stepped around him, out of the office, and closed the door behind her.

"You need to do something about her," Derrick said, coming forward into the office. "The next client may not be as understanding."

Noelle came around the desk, meeting him halfway. She gestured to the sofa on the other side of the room. "Terri is indispensable to me. So I suggest you reconcile yourself to dealing with her if you plan to continue this."

Derrick, startled by the sharp retort, glanced at

Noelle. His sinister smile appeared briefly. "Nice try. You won't get rid of me that fast."

"Didn't think so, but I had to try," she muttered. "Have a seat." She gestured to the sofa and the television sitting on a media cart in front of it.

Derrick obediently crossed the room and, unbuttoning his jacket, took a seat. "Did you like the flowers?"

Noelle took a seat on the opposite end of the sofa and picked up the remote sitting on the small, oak side table nearby. "Yes. Thank you," she answered quickly, hoping that would be the end of it. Of course, it was not.

"Wasn't sure what you like, so I just told them a mixed bouquet."

She clicked the on button. "The unique thing about Love Unlimited, Mr. Brandt, is not one particular way of matching couples, such as video interviews, speed dating, et cetera. What's unique is the way we take all the available resources and combine them for maximum results."

"So, what do you like?"

"I beg your pardon?"

"Flowers? What kind of flowers do you like?"

Noelle considered not answering but had a feeling that would only make him more determined to know. "Sunflowers."

"Sunflowers. I should've known your choice in flowers would be as unique as everything else about you."

Uh-oh. Noelle's eyes flashed to his to confirm her suspicion. In that instant, Noelle realized just what message the flowers were suppose to send, and it had nothing to do with a truce. The *ogler* was back.

"I've compiled several video interviews from some of our most promising candidates. I would like to review the tapes with you, if that is all right." She turned on the DVD player, and a pretty young woman appeared on the screen.

Derrick frowned. "How old is that little girl?"

"Twenty-three," Noelle answered, a bit taken aback by his obvious displeasure.

"Twenty-three my ass. You're trying to hook me up with jailbait?"

"She's a legal adult, I assure you. Just take a look at her video."

"Why? There's nothing there." He huffed dismissively. "Go on to the next one."

Noelle could feel the anger swelling in her chest, but she fought it back. The last thing she needed to do was go off on this man, no matter how much he may have deserved it.

She turned to face Derrick on the sofa. "Okay, we need to get something straight." She pointed her index finger at him. "I will not tolerate your cavalier attitude toward these women. The way you treated Suzanne last week was reprehensible! I will not, *will not,* send you on a date with a single candidate if you cannot conduct yourself in a civilized manner and as a gentleman."

The pair sat staring at each other for several seconds as an uncomfortable silence descended on the room.

Finally, Derrick grinned. "You're such a beautiful woman. Are you seeing anyone?"

The cap on her volcano popped. She was on her feet. "And that's another thing! I don't know what kind of agency you think I'm running here, but I am *not* a part of the service."

"Hold up." Derrick put up both hands defensively. "That is not what I meant."

She placed her hands on her hips. "I know what you

meant. But despite my financial troubles, I am still running a respectable business. Do you understand?"

His green eyes watched her for so long that Noelle began to feel a little squeamish. Realizing she was still on her feet, she sat suddenly. "Now…can we get back to the videos?"

His lips firmly pressed together, Derrick gestured for her to continue.

Three hours and many, many profiles later, they were no closer to finding an acceptable match. Derrick had rejected each and every candidate for one reason or another.

Hanging on to the tip of her final nerve, Noelle turned off the DVD player and turned to face Derrick. She slowly placed the remote on the table, hoping the additional moments would give her some restraint.

Taking a deep breath, she quickly rehearsed the proper, respectful words to convey her thoughts in her head once, twice, and then opened her mouth to speak.

"What the hell is wrong with you?"

"Me?" Obviously, Derrick had been expecting the explosion, because he came right back. "I gave you a long list of very specific requirements, and none of those women fit my requirements."

Noelle's eyes widened in amazement. "What *long* list? You said big breasts and a sturdy pelvis. How the hell would I know if a woman has a sturdy pelvis?"

"I'll show you." In a flash, Derrick was off the sofa, and with two steps in her direction he reached down and snatched Noelle up off the couch. His large hands fastened on to her hips and yanked her forward until they were pressed body to body.

Before Noelle's brain had time to even process that,

he was kissing her. And much to her amazement, she was kissing him back.

Lord, he tasted good! *Like a cinnamon bun,* Noelle thought dreamily as she parted her lips and allowed his warm tongue inside. Of their own volition, her arms slid up and over his broad shoulders, and she discovered he was just the right height for her to rest comfortably against him. Most of the men she dated tended to be several inches shorter than she was.

In response, Noelle was unable to resist the soft sigh that escaped from her mouth. His tongue darted out and ran over her bottom lip in a slow, sensual glide, and Noelle felt her knees weaken.

But his strong hands bunched in the material of her skirt at each hip, holding her up and against him. She couldn't have fallen if she'd wanted to. Feeling the growing warmth pressing against her center, Noelle knew she should end the kiss, end the touching. This was wrong...so wrong.

But all she could do was allow her head to fall back as his soft lips left a trail of kisses from her chin to her collarbone. Her heartbeat sped up as she felt him grinding his growing erection against her. She couldn't have lied to herself if she'd wanted to. The feeling was mutual, and she spontaneously began to meet his grind with her own.

"Oh," he moaned against her ear. "Oh, damn."

Noelle felt the earth shift and realized she was suddenly on her back on the sofa. The sudden motion seemed to shake her loose from the magical spell he had cast around her.

Instantly, she was kicking and scratching as if her very life depended on it. Derrick rolled away from her onto the floor, and Noelle jumped off the couch and rushed across the room to put the desk between them.

Her heart was still pounding; she had no idea what to say. She fully understood that she was as guilty as he. She closed her eyes, trying to force away the memory of his hot, heavy body and the realization that she was already missing it.

When she finally opened her eyes, Derrick was still on the other side of the room. Sitting with his back against the couch, one leg stretched out and another at an angle, and the bold evidence of his arousal was still quite obvious.

He was staring at her in that same unreadable way, and she could only imagine what he saw. The shocked and offended professional. Or the woman who wanted to go to him even now and finish what they'd started.

Slowly, he rose to his feet, wincing slightly. He dusted his pants off and buttoned his jacket. "I'll expect to hear from you within a week with a list of women who fit my criteria."

And as calm as a king dismissing a subject, he crossed the room and walked out, leaving the door open in his wake.

Once again, Noelle blindly reached for her chair and plopped down into it. One thing had become patently obvious. The usual methods would not work with Derrick Brandt. For this man, she was going to have to reinvent the wheel. She only hoped he would take it and drive away, far away from her.

Chapter 7

"I don't know all the exact details, but it has something to do with the planets aligning or something like that. Anyway, on that date the world will end." The pleasingly plump Catherine Zeta-Jones look-alike sitting across from him giggled gleefully. "Of course, I don't believe any of that stuff, but it's still interesting, don't you think? That all these calendars have that date in com—"

A loud, startling bell interrupted her.

Thank God! Derrick forced a pleasant smile and tried to ignore the disappointed look on her face as she shrugged sweetly. It was, Derrick thought, the first appealing thing she'd done since sitting down across from him at the Love Unlimited speed dating mixer exactly twelve minutes ago.

"Nice meeting you," she said and promptly hopped up as another beautiful woman took the seat. The fifth of the evening, and all Derrick could think about was the moderator standing on the other side of the room. With that stupid little bell dangling from her lovely fingers.

The bell rang, and for the fourth time Derrick fought down the overwhelming urge to cross the room and snatch it out of her hand. Who did she think she was fooling anyway? Derrick knew he was as heavy on her mind as she was on his.

"Derrick," he answered in response to the question being asked by the current buxom beauty sitting across from him. "Nice to meet you, Brenda."

The women being presented to him tonight only reinforced what he already believed. Noelle, recognizing his attraction to her, had lined up women that in some way resembled her. As if she could simply redirect his lust. *Sorry, sweet. Despite their physical resemblance, there is not a single other woman like you here tonight.*

Derrick caught the tail end of what Brenda was saying and felt his temper flare. "Well, don't believe everything you read in the papers."

"Oh, don't get me wrong." Her brown eyes sparkled with something he couldn't quite put his finger on. "I like a passionate man. A little aggression is good for a relationship. So, did you hurt her?" she asked with a sinister smile.

"What?"

"Your girlfriend, the one you caught with that other guy? I saw the picture of you dragging her out of the club. You must have been humiliated, huh?" She leaned forward, and Derrick suddenly realized the sparkle in her eyes was excitement. "When you got home, did you *punish* her?"

Oh, hell no! Derrick stood from his chair. "Enough of this nonsense."

He headed across the room toward Noelle, ignoring the interested expressions on the faces of the men and women at the tables spread throughout the restaurant.

Noelle, seeing what was happening, moved to intercept him. "Mr. Brandt, is there a problem?"

Derrick plucked the bell from her fingers and slung it across the room. "Come with me."

"But—I don't understand. What's wrong? I'm sure we can straighten it out—just tell me what happened."

Seeing that Derrick had no intention of releasing her or explaining, she called back over her shoulder. "Terri, find the bell. It's all right, everyone. Please continue. I'll be back shortly."

Derrick headed toward a set of swinging doors he thought might lead to the restaurant's kitchen, not really sure where he was going, only knowing he desperately needed to be alone with her.

"You have no right to kidnap me like this!" she hissed at him.

"After what you put me through tonight, don't you dare try to tell me about what's right," he hissed back.

Pushing open the swinging doors revealed a large, brightly lit kitchen. There was no one around so the staff must have been on break. Once the doors swung closed, and they were out of view of her clients, Noelle jerked hard and pulled away from him.

She darted around a stainless-steel preparation table and, leaning forward, glared at him. "You psychotic jackass! You're completely out of control! What was I thinking taking you on as a client? You're insane! Completely insane!"

Despite the tirade of insults spewing from her lovely lips, Derrick felt an overwhelming sense of calm come over him. This was exactly what he'd wanted all night: to be alone in a room with her.

She was so damn sexy. She had to know what she looked like, dressed in a snug fitting leopard-print dress that bunched provocatively at the hips. The low-cut V-neck that gave one of those tempting glimpses of cleavage that only made a man want to see more.

Her black hair falling in feminine ringlets around her pretty face. Her soft brown eyes practically glowing with fury. She was incredible—and as hot for him as he was for her.

If Camille seriously thought he was strong enough to just walk away from this marvelous creation of God, Derrick thought, she obviously gave him far more credit than he deserved.

He started around the preparation station toward her, and Noelle quickly darted in the other direction. "Uh-uh—I remember that look." She edged away from him, watching to counter his movements. "No, Derrick! No kissing! I mean it!"

Derrick grinned. She didn't mean it. He could hear her heart calling to his from across the room. "You look beautiful tonight, Noelle. Did you wear that dress to please me?"

"You arrogant ass!" she shouted. "I wouldn't wear a potato sack to please you!"

Derrick resisted the urge to smile as her eyes widened with the realization that everyone in the other room had probably heard that. He made a *tsking* sound. "Temper, temper."

Suddenly the swinging doors opened and Terri stood

there glaring at Derrick. Two of Noelle's male clients were standing just behind Terri, surveying the scene.

"Everything okay, Noelle?" Terri asked.

Derrick's eyes darted from the two men to Noelle. Time for truth or dare. If she truly wanted to be rid of him, she'd seek the comfort of her rescue team, and he would end the night by fighting his way out of here or…

"Everything's fine, Terri. Sorry to alarm you." Her tight smile did not fool anyone. She was fighting down some seriously strong emotions.

The people in the doorway probably assumed it was anger, but Derrick was certain it was passion. Either way, she had not thrown him to the wolves as she could have so conveniently done, which only encouraged his growing assertiveness.

"You sure?" Terri's hard eyes were still firmly on Derrick.

"Yes, I'm fine." Derrick could hear Noelle's attempt to infuse confidence into her voice. He wondered if she realized she was giving up her last chance to get rid of him.

The three slowly drifted back into the other room, leaving Derrick and Noelle standing at opposite ends of the preparation table.

"Look, Derrick, I understand you're attracted to me, and…as much as I hate to admit it, I'm obviously attracted to you. But it would never work."

"Why not?"

"You mean other than the fact that you make me crazy?"

"Yes, other than that."

"How can I explain this…. See, I specialize in putting people together who have compatible personalities. It's what I do, seeking out people who fit together in the best possible way. I know what I need in a man, and—not to be insulting, but you're not it."

"How can you be so sure?"

"This is a perfect example." She gestured to the table between them. "This chasing me around a table. We're fully grown adults, for goodness' sake. This is ludicrous and incredibly undignified."

Derrick could not suppress the grin that formed on his lips. "Baby, I haven't even begun to show you undignified."

"The point is, this kind of unseemly behavior is not something I enjoy. Although, granted, I'm sure there are women who would love this kind of ardent attention. I'm just not one of them."

"So, your ideal man would never chase you around a table?"

"Of course not."

"That's easy enough to fix. Stop running, and I'll stop chasing."

"You're deliberately missing the point." She threw up her hands in surrender. "There's no reasoning with you. Just know this—Derrick Brandt, it ain't ever gonna happen. So let it go." She headed toward the doors, and it was just the opportunity Derrick had been waiting for.

He quickly intersected her path, scooped her up in his arms and carried her to a darkened area in the back of the kitchen.

"Put me—" was all she managed to get out before his mouth came down heavily on hers. The darkened area turned out to be the dishwashing sink. Derrick gently sat her on the ledge of the double sink, his lips never leaving hers.

"Oh," she groaned painfully, "what are you doing to me?"

Derrick felt her arms wrap around his shoulders, and she pulled him closer into her body. She felt so good. Better than he remembered as he made a place for himself between her spread thighs. Even through the layers of clothing separating them, he could feel the fever building in her center. She was on fire!

He couldn't take her on a kitchen sink…could he? No! No—he could wait…but maybe just a taste.

Derrick buried his head against her neck, fighting for control as she lifted her hips, allowing him to sink deeper into her. "Baby, I'm trying real hard not to do anything *undignified,* but you're not making it easy."

Lost in her own pleasure, she continued to lift her hips, rocking back and forth against him. Her head lolled to the side, exposing her soft, vulnerable neck to his kisses.

The scent of paradise floated into his nose as his mouth took an extended tour of her chin and neck, down into the valley of her wonderful cleavage.

His large hands came up to outline her full bust, his thumbs stroking over her nipples until she was revealed to him through the thin material of the dress. He started to lower his mouth to taste, but stopped.

She would never forgive him if he sent her back to her guests in a dress with a damp bust line. Instead, he quickly reached around and slid the zipper halfway down, just enough to slip the dress off her shoulders.

It slid down her smooth, silky shoulders until her full, ripe breasts were exposed to him. His cupped her in his trembling hands. "You're perfect. You're—"

Deciding he could better show her than tell her, his

hungry mouth came down on first one breast, then the other, feasting and feeding the beast within him. The beast that even now demanded he find some way to possess her forever.

Derrick knew somewhere deep inside his brain, where logic still fought for control, that he needed to stop this before it got out of hand. But how could he when she was grinding against his erection so eagerly? Who was he to deny this beautiful woman what she obviously wanted?

Still suckling on her breasts, his large hand slid under her dress. The soft material slid up her thigh easily. He needed to stop this. Really…he needed to…

His hands came to his zipper. As he began to slide the zipper down, even as he struggled failingly to resist the pull against his compulsive nature, he heard the door open.

"Noelle?" The sound of Terri's worried voice was like being doused in cold water. "Noelle, where are you?"

Noelle felt a shiver of fear run up her spine. She opened her eyes to find Derrick's green eyes practically glowing in the dim light. His large body was hunkered over hers. His heart was pounding against her. One warm hand was on her thigh and the other was somewhere between their bodies. She could feel his hard knuckles against her center and used every ounce of her being to resist the throbbing she was helpless to control.

"I'm fine, Terri. I'll be right there."

"People are starting to ask questions."

"I'll be right there." She fought to control the trembling coursing through her core, but, like the throbbing, it was out of her hands.

A few seconds later, they heard the swinging door close.

Derrick's mouth came down on hers again, but this time she forced herself to turn her head away. "Stop," she whispered, hoping he would believe it.

He didn't. "That's not what you want."

Her eyes narrowed. "How would you know what I want?"

She swallowed as the hand between them shifted position, and he was suddenly cupping her hot spot. "She tells me everything I need to know."

"It's like that, huh?"

He frowned. "What are you talking about?"

"Go ahead, do it." She pushed her body against his hand. "It's what you want, isn't it? Take it—and then get the hell out of my life!"

He let go of her as if she had suddenly caught fire. Backing up against the opposite wall. "I'm not like that, Noelle."

She quickly slipped her bra and dress back into place and stood on wobbly legs. "Glad to hear it." She struggled to zip her dress and silently wondered how she could face the roomful of people she'd brought together tonight.

As she worked to get her appearance back to something resembling normal, he simply stood, giving her that stare she was growing to hate.

"You are some piece of work, lady," he finally said with the shake of his head.

Once she was as comfortable as she could be, Noelle turned and headed back into the kitchen. She could feel Derrick on her heels but refused to give him the satisfaction of speeding up or acknowledging his presence in any way.

At the double doors, she paused, losing her nerve.

Suddenly Derrick burst past her. "Fine, Ms. Brown,

but I expect results or else I want my money back!" With that he stormed angrily through the restaurant, as everyone turned to watch him leave.

When he reached the front entrance of the restaurant, he turned in her direction and shouted, "And the next time, you will not talk me out of it!" Then he disappeared through the doors.

Everyone turned to look at her, and Noelle felt suddenly cold with embarrassment—and relief.

With his explosive exit, Derrick, in his own clumsy way, had tried to protect her reputation, leading everyone to believe they'd been arguing the entire time—when they'd actually been doing anything but. From the looks on people's faces, it had worked.

"Sorry for the interruption, everyone. Please, let's continue. Enjoy yourselves, and one another." Outside of a few stray looks, everyone returned to their conversations.

Noelle did her best to look relaxed and composed and to keep her mind off the constant throbbing between her legs. She could only hope the evening would end soon. Because she was not sure how much longer she could sit there and pretend every part of her being was not aching for a man who was impossible to deal with.

How much longer could she be the composed professional they expected and not the aching woman she was? How much longer could she resist Derrick Brandt's magical touch?

Chapter 8

Noelle continued typing on the computer, ignoring the telephone ringing in the background. Finally, after the tenth ring, it stopped.

Noelle breathed a sigh of relief until she glanced at the phone and saw the message light had come on. He'd left a message. It was the first time he'd done that.

It was Saturday morning. Terri was off, and few people would even know she was in the office. So when the phone started ringing that morning, she'd thought it odd—until she saw the name on the caller ID.

Noelle had almost instantly regretted her lusty behavior with Derrick Brandt the night before. She had hoped that if she just avoided him, the issue might go away on its own. Apparently, Derrick wasn't about to let that happen.

He'd started calling bright and early and had continued all day. Around noon, she finally accepted that he would not give up, but by then she'd also decided that her initial impression of him had been correct. He was way too aggressive for her taste, and he was not a man used to being denied something he wanted. Now he'd left a message, and she was dying to hear it.

She shook off the impulse and returned to work. That blinking light seem to haunt her until she couldn't stand it anymore. She picked up the receiver and typed in the code to receive her message. The message was short and concise.

"It's Derrick. We need to talk about last night."

She frowned at the phone. He sounded so reasonable and normal. It was hard to compare the voice on the phone with the man who'd insulted Suzanne, or chased her around the table in the restaurant, or carried her to the back of the restaurant and…

In truth, it wasn't just *his* behavior that bothered her. She glanced at the couch on the other side of the room, remembering what had transpired there while they were reviewing profiles. Noelle knew that she would only be lying to herself to say that she was not attracted to Derrick Brandt. Apparently, she was extremely attracted to him, to the point where her usual sound reasoning seemed to fly right out the window whenever he touched her.

There was something about Derrick Brandt that brought out her primal woman. Something about the mesmerizing quality of those lovely green eyes made her want to get naked and stay that way for as long as he wanted.

That was the real danger. Her lack of self-control where this one man was concerned. Noelle was no Virgin Mary, but compared to her small circle of girlfriends, she'd led a somewhat cloistered life. She'd dated off and on throughout the years, but the relationships had always been well-thought-out, rational relationships. Not random heated encounters in the backs of restaurants.

In fact, the last relationship she'd had was with a legal-brief fact-checker, and when the passion—what little there was—had fizzled out, they'd parted amicably.

Somehow Noelle knew there would never be an amicable breakup with Derrick Brandt. His previous track record proved that he was incapable of that. The last thing she needed in her life right now was a hot, heated love affair with a high-profile character who had a habit of dramatic, public breakups.

No, Noelle was a woman who prided herself on her sound, good judgment and conservative lifestyle. Even as a child, she'd been the quiet one. Oftentimes, she'd been forced to mediate conflicts between her siblings. Everyone knew what to expect from Noelle, and she liked that. She was dependable, predictable and moderate in most things. Even total strangers seemed to pick up on this part of her personality in a short time, which was why she'd never once been passed over for jury duty.

So why didn't Derrick Brandt seem to understand that? He apparently had mistaken her for some kind of wild weekend romp. Of course, her behavior up until now must've only confirmed his belief.

All he had to do was give her a hard stare and her clothes started falling off. She understood the primary reason for his intense pursuit. Derrick wanted to finish what they'd started in her office and in the restaurant. Quite frankly, so did she.

This was all the more reason why she had to avoid him. At least until she could come up with a better strategy. The deposit he'd put down was already spent, so there was no way she could just drop him as a client.

Somehow, she had to get his focus back on his reasons for coming to Love Unlimited in the first place and off the crazy, undeniable chemistry between them. That meant no physical contact whatsoever, at least for now.

For now, she had a ton of work to get done and not a lot of time. The twins were in a pageant that evening, and she wanted to get finished in time to attend.

The phone started ringing again, and Noelle decided to temporarily pull the cord from the wall. She knew she would have to face him eventually, but it was too soon. The feel of his warm, callused hands on her body was still too fresh in her memory. His wonderfully masculine smell was still in her nose, his sensually seductive words still in her ears, and she simply could not trust herself to be reasonable where Derrick Brandt was concerned. And that was a most frightening realization.

Across town in the Massey Building, Derrick hung up the desk phone and grabbed his suede jacket off the back of his chair. "Camille, can you finish this up without me?" he asked, referring to the pile of employee evaluations they were reviewing together.

"No. Where are you going?" She frowned up at him.

Derrick gave her a knowing look; she was the one who had taught him how to do evaluations. "Well, then it has to wait until I get back. I have to run out."

"I gave up my Saturday to come in here and help you with these, and now you're leaving? And you promised me dinner!"

"I'll be back in plenty of time for dinner. But the 'evals' will have to wait. I have to take care of something."

"What is more important than your business?"

"According to you, my nonexistent love life."

Her eyes brightened considerably. "Oh? Is this about the matchmaker?"

"Yes, and before you ask another question, don't." He grabbed his keys off the edge of his desk and headed toward the office door.

"Fine by me, if you want to make a jackass of yourself with the only woman who's stirred your interest in over a year."

Derrick was almost to the door when he stopped. "What do you mean, make a jackass of myself?" He couldn't help noticing she'd chosen Noelle's favorite nickname for him.

"I assume that's who you've been calling all morning. But you think she is intentionally avoiding you?"

"Yes."

"Why?"

"That's none of your business. What's this about making a jackass of myself?"

"Hmm." She reclined in her high-back chair and watched him with studious eyes. "What could you have done? From what you've told me, she obviously needs your business. She is not going to risk angering an important client over any minor infraction. So it had to be something big. Hmm."

Derrick crossed the distance to the door and pushed it closed before leaning his back against it. "I may have…tried to make out with her in a restaurant kitchen."

Camille's eyes widened, but she said nothing.

"It's her own fault. It was a mixer for her clients, and

she wore this sexy leopard-print dress. I just wanted to snatch it off her."

"Derrick!"

"Sorry, sometimes I forget you're not a man."

"So I assume, being you, you did try to snatch it off her?"

"More or less."

"Oh, Derrick, what am I going to do with you?" She shook her head. "How many times have I tried to explain to you that you can't just take what you want because you want it? And that includes women.

"Derrick, I don't want to discourage you, but maybe you shouldn't have such a negative attitude about dating and finding love. Isn't that what you went to this agency for? Why not just go into it with an open mind and see what happens? If it doesn't work out—okay. But to go with the attitude that you are not going to even try just seems a bit closed minded."

"Why waste time with other women when I can have the one I want?"

"Can you have the one you want? Seems to me that's your problem, Derrick. You always want what you can't have. Think about your choices in women. Always women you had to chase down. Or, if you didn't have to chase them, they were up to no good to begin with. I just don't want to see you get hurt again chasing after this matchmaker."

There was nothing he could say in response. As usual, Camille's logic was indisputable. Maybe he was just setting himself up for another disappointment.

It had always been this way. Maybe it was the remnants of a child deprived too long, or maybe it was just simply greed. Derrick had never been able to restrain himself from his own desires. Not when the craving was strong enough.

When something pulled at that deep hunger in his belly, Derrick was powerless to resist, even when the greatest odds seemed against it. His very life was a testament to this fact.

Derrick was silent, not knowing how to explain to Camille the deep hunger that he seemed never able to satisfy. That gnawing at his soul that occurred when something he desired greatly seemed within reach and yet unattainable. It was his greatest motivation, the driving force behind his success. Most people called it ambition or determination, but Derrick knew it was something bigger than both those things.

It was the culmination of a lifetime of deprivation. It was the starving child who could never get full. The thirsty man who could never drink his fill. It was a deeply inherited part of him, not something he could throw on and off at will.

It was also his greatest downfall. It was that feeling of failure, the sharp taste of defeat when he'd finally obtained the unattainable only to discover it was not what he'd thought. Waking up the morning after with a woman he'd thought he could love forever only to discover he'd been deceived by the illusion of lust. Because of the hunger in his heart, he spent a great deal of his time chasing ghosts.

And since there was no way to explain the overall phenomenon that had plagued his life, there was an even smaller chance of making Camille understand how meeting Noelle Brown had intensified that hunger to a breaking point.

Touching her had been every bit as satisfying as he'd

known it would. Noelle Brown was the real deal; he knew it in his soul. Being with her had the sublime feeling of finally arriving at a long-sought destination. She was the right place. And he could not, would not, let her slip through his fingers.

Camille was right about one thing; his inability to control his own nature. His swift temper had cost him both publicly and in his private relationships. He could not take that chance with Noelle.

"So, if you were me, what would you do?"

Camille smiled. "I would listen to my older, wiser business partner. You know, the one that was happily married to the love of her life for forty years."

Derrick crossed the room and retook his seat. "Okay, older, wiser business partner, I'm listening."

Chapter 9

"Excuse me, excuse me." Noelle worked her way down the row of proud parents, grandparents, and various other family members, trying to reach her own. "Pardon me, excuse me."

She finally reached the seat next to her sister, Kimber. "Thanks for holding it."

"What took you so long?" Kimber asked, removing the coat she'd laid over the seat.

"Got hung up at the office," she whispered, settling into her seat. She shielded her eyes, trying to see past the bright lights to the performers on the stage. "Where are they?"

Kimber shielded her own eyes. "Fairies three and four on the left. They're *all* Tinkerbell! More fairy than flash of light."

Noelle grinned, finding her twin nieces on the stage.

"Oh, they are so adorable! I've got to get a picture of them in those outfits."

"Don't worry, Mom took enough to fill an album." Kimber glanced at her sister. "Where were you today? I tried calling your office like twelve times."

Noelle kept her eyes on the stage. "Sorry, I was around, just really busy. So, how much did I miss?"

"Only about twenty minutes. You okay?"

"Yeah, why?"

"I don't know. You seem weird—*weirder* than normal."

"Ha-ha."

"Shh," someone called from the back.

"You'd think this was a Broadway production of *Madame Butterfly,*" Kimber whispered, but they both quieted.

Apparently, all of those phone calls had not been Derrick. Noelle still hadn't decided how to deal with him.

Not answering your phone was not a smart way to run a business, but nothing to do with Derrick Brandt had been handled with anything resembling smarts. What had she been thinking? Allowing him to touch her so…so…

She still felt mortified remembering how easily she'd given in to his advances.

If anyone had told her she could succumb so easily to a man she barely knew, she would've denied it completely. But the warmth she still felt at his remembered touch was all the proof she needed.

Almost an hour later, the production of *Peter Pan* ended and the row of preschoolers took a grand bow before the crowd. The Browns hooted and howled with pride, and Noelle was so lost in her own thoughts that she didn't even experience the usual embarrassment at her family's antics.

Twenty minutes later, Noelle, her parents, Claudia and

Gil, her sister, Kimber, her brother, Ray, and his wife, Ann, along with their twin daughters, Lea and Lena, were settling into a celebratory dinner at Dmitri's Upstairs, an upscale family restaurant in the university center.

The guests of honor, having refused to change out of their fairy costumes, were drawing flattering attention from the other restaurant patrons, and they basked in every moment of glory.

"Good evening, everyone." Their waiter, a young Asian man, approached the table. "How is everyone tonight?"

"I'm a fairy!" Lea announced proudly.

"Me, too!" Lena chirped. Scrambling to her knees, she quickly stood on her seat to show off her pink leotard and chiffon tutu. "See?"

"Lena, sit down." Ray used his stern voice.

With a pouty bottom lip, Lena obeyed her father and plopped down on her diapered bottom.

After ordering, Kimber clinked her glass with her fork. "I have an announcement." Kimber took a deep breath and looked at each of her family members.

"I was offered a promotion today."

The table exploded in congratulations and applause.

"Wait, there's more." She put up her hand to halt the praise. "The job is at our corporate office in Los Angeles, California."

"California!" Claudia immediately began to shake her head frantically. "No, no, you are not moving to California."

The three siblings exchanged smiles. Sometimes their mother forgot the fact that they were all now adults.

"What kind of job is it, pumpkin?" Gil was much more subdued than his wife, but Noelle knew it was just a cover for the deep emotions that ran just beneath his calm facade.

"Chief financial officer," Kimber boasted proudly. "And…" She paused, waiting for her excited family to calm down. "I get an expense account, a six-figure salary, a company car and a corner office. They even move me for free."

"Whoa!" Gil sat back in his chair. "Who knew the plumbing, bathroom and kitchen supply and design business could be so lucrative?" The table exploded in applause and congratulations.

Noelle picked up a bread stick from the basket in the middle of the table and concentrated on buttering it as her family members continued to pepper Kimber with questions about her new job. This had not been a good week. And this certainly was not the news she wanted to end it on.

Noelle, Kimber and Ray were only a year apart in age and had been almost inseparable as children. Outside of the typical sibling disputes, they had always gotten along surprisingly well. Into their adult years, they'd still been a large part of each other's day-to-day lives. So the idea that her sister was moving to the other side of the country was not a welcome change.

"Excuse me, ladies' room." Noelle stood and quickly walked away from the table. As she wound her way through the tables, she heard snippets of the excited conversation behind her as her family continued to pepper Kimber with questions.

She headed down the stairs to the bathroom on the lower level where the entrance was located. *What a lousy week.* She sniffled, reaching the bottom. She turned the corner toward the entrance and ran smack-dab into a wide chest.

Strong hands reached out to steady her, and as she

lifted her eyes to apologize to the stranger, Noelle suddenly realized that her lousy week was about to get worse.

Derrick's eyes widened in surprise as he looked down at the woman who'd bumped into him. He was holding Noelle Brown.

And she looked so sad.

His heart clenched in his chest to see tears in those soft, brown eyes he'd spent too much time thinking about over the past week. The last time he'd looked into those eyes, they'd been filled with fire and passion. Now there was only melancholy.

"What's wrong?"

Noelle was instantly torn as to how to greet him. The last time she'd seen him, she'd been half-naked and panting with lust. Despite their last parting, it was time to put their relationship back on a professional footing.

"Mr. Brandt, what a surprise." She tried to pull away, but he held her upper arms firmly, trying not to tighten his grip too much. "If you'll excuse me, I was just on my way to the ladies' room."

"Did you get my messages today?" Derrick growled.

"Derrick?" Camille whispered from beside him.

Derrick suddenly remembered that he was not alone. "Camille, this is Noelle Brown. The owner of Love Unlimited."

While he was distracted, Noelle twisted her body in a way that he could not quickly compensate for and slipped through his fingers. "It was nice seeing you—good evening to you both." With only a brief glance at his companion, she hurried away down the hall, and Derrick turned to go after her until Camille's sharp words stopped him.

"Derrick!" She thumped her cane on the floor. "Have you completely forgotten what we discussed earlier?"

"No, but I can't just let her go like that!" he snapped louder than he meant to, but he was concerned about Noelle and still thought he should go after her. "I need to talk to her. I need to find out who upset her." He watched as she disappeared into the ladies' room.

"Do you even *hear* yourself when you talk?" Camille was frowning up at him. "And if she told you why she's upset, what would you do?"

His eyes narrowed on the restroom door. "Make sure they never did it again."

"Derrick, listen to yourself. You can't just demand!" She touched his sleeve. "Remember what we discussed earlier? Kindness, Derrick. Gentleness. That's what she needs right now, not you snarling and demanding answers."

"Mr. Brandt, are you ready to be seated?" An older maitre d' stood patiently to the side.

Derrick glanced at the man. "Yes, can you please seat Mrs. Massey. I'll be along in a moment."

"Yes, sir." The maitre d' gestured for Camille to follow, but she ignored him and stayed right where she was, staring up at Derrick.

"Remember what we talked about." She reached up and ran a hand over his stubbled cheek. "If you're ever to have what you want most, you've got to learn to control your emotions."

The maitre d' gave a not-so-discreet cough to regain their attention. Derrick would've probably been embarrassed to have the man witnessing this scene if most of his attention hadn't already been divided between what Camille was saying and the image of Noelle's sad eyes.

* * *

A few minutes later, Noelle hesitantly emerged from the ladies' room to find Derrick Brandt leaning against the opposite wall.

"You okay?" he asked.

"Yes." She glanced down the hall. "Where's your friend?"

"She's no friend."

"She seemed like a friend."

"More like a conscience. And my business partner."

The pair stood opposite each other as an awkward silence descended.

"We need to discuss what happened the other night." His deep voice resonated in the narrow corridor.

"No, we don't." She started to walk away.

As she passed, Derrick grabbed her forearm. Even through the thin material of her blouse, his warm hand heated her flesh and brought back all the sensual memories of their last encounter.

"Yes. We do."

"You know we can never have anything but a professional relationship."

"No, I don't know that."

"You're my client, Derrick. I don't date my clients."

"I don't get it. The whole purpose of your business is to find soul mates for people. So why not yourself?"

She huffed. "You are *not* my soul mate."

"How can you be so sure?"

"You can't be serious!" She glanced into his green eyes and saw not a hint of sarcastic humor. "You only want to go out with me because you think I'm…easy."

He laughed, a full-bodied laugh that sounded like music to her ears. Noelle forced herself to remain stone-faced. This man could slip beneath her defenses so quickly.

"Trust me, beautiful, you're anything but easy."

"I won't sleep with you, Derrick. You need to understand that right now. I'm not running some kinda call-girl service."

"Why do you keep saying things like that? I've never made that accusation."

"You won't have to. Others will."

"Is that what you're worried about? What other people will think?"

"What do you think will be said when it gets out that you're dating the owner of a dating agency?"

"That I'm dating the owner of a dating agency. What do *you* think will be said?"

"That the media will call Love Unlimited something other than a matchmaking service."

"Noelle, I have no control over the media. Only my own actions, and I can't live my life concerned about bad reporting."

"Spoken like a man who has nothing to lose," she said with a shake of her head. "I, on the other hand, have everything to lose."

"You think I have nothing to lose?" His eyes widened. "I could lose you."

"You have no idea if we would work or not!"

"Exactly. I only know what my gut tells me." He stepped closer, careful not to touch her. "And my gut tells me that what I experienced the other night, what *we* experienced…was only a *glimpse* of what is possible. There is something magical here, Noelle. Are you not even the slightest bit curious about this magic between us?"

She huffed. "It's not magic. Just lust."

He smiled his wolfish smile. "That, too." He glanced down the hallway to make sure they were still alone before his strong arm snaked around her waist and pulled her to him. "I tell you what—"

"Let me go!" She instantly started to squirm.

"Just listen a minute."

"Let me—"

Instead of releasing her, his arms tightened and his soft lips came down hard on hers.

Without hesitation, Noelle's arms wrapped around his neck as her lips parted under his assault. She felt her whole body give a great sigh of relief. How she'd missed his touch. It felt like it had been a lifetime. She greedily met his tongue with her own as he explored her hungry mouth. She shifted her body to press closer to him, trying in her deepest core to become one body with him. Right and wrong, good and bad—none of the usual laws of the universe applied when she was in his arms. All that mattered was the incredible feeling of satisfaction she felt coursing through ever cell of her being. And right now she needed this more than ever.

Derrick broke the kiss first. "Give me three dates to change your mind." His soft lips placed gentle kisses along her neck between words. "Three dates of my choosing, and if you do not feel we have what it takes, I'll leave you alone."

Noelle, with her head laid back in surrender to his gentle persuasions, wasn't even capable of thinking, let alone complicated reasoning. All she wanted was for it to never end.

"Three dates, Noelle." His tongue slinked up behind her ear, and she gripped his shirtsleeves to stay on her feet. "What do you say?"

"Oh, yes, yes." Her hand maneuvered between their bodies as she cupped his growing erection.

"Hmm. Don't start what you can't finish. What do you say?"

Suddenly remembering where they were, she glanced up and down the corridor. "You know this is a mistake."

"Is that a yes?" he persisted.

She glanced at him, and he smiled. That bad-boy smile that had left such an impression the first time they met. That smile she both loved and hated. It was startling to realize that first meeting had occurred only a few weeks ago. So why did it feel like she'd known this man her whole life? That he knew just how to comfort her?

"I have a proposition for you," she said, crossing her arms over her chest, now feeling fully in control of herself again. "I'll give you three dates, if you give me three dates."

"What do you mean?"

"In between each of our dates, you go out with a woman I recommend based on my client profiles."

"And what exactly is that supposed to achieve?"

"Well…I guess three things really. One, diversity. Two, a comparative analysis. And three…" She hesitated, not sure exactly how to say what she was thinking.

"Three?" he prompted.

"Let's just say I would rather not have all your concentrated sexual energy focused on me—exclusively."

He grinned. "Too late for that. Nonetheless, I agree to your terms. Starting with dinner with you tomorrow night. Agreed?" He extended his hand, and she took it.

His grin widened, and Noelle instantly began to suspect that she'd made a deal with her own sexy, personal devil.

Chapter 10

By three o'clock the next afternoon, Noelle was *certain* she'd made a bad bargain.

Derrick called and told her that he would send a car to pick her up for their dinner date that night. For the hundredth time she considered canceling, but as much as she did not want to admit it, a large part of her was very much looking forward to it.

When the chauffeured Lexus pulled up in front of her brownstone at six o'clock exactly, Noelle was sitting at her desk which overlooked the street below. She'd spent most of the day working feverishly to find Derrick a viable candidate based on the information in his file, but the effort was proving more difficult than she'd imagined. Suzanne really was her best candidate, and thanks to Derrick that was no longer a possibility.

She'd dressed in a foam-green, sequined top with

thin spaghetti straps, matching silk pants and beaded wrap and stiletto heels, along with her wool and fur coat. Noelle had received many compliments on the outfit when she wore it and knew it was very flattering to her unique body style, but she refused to stop and examine why she'd chosen it, not wanting to admit to any desire to look her best tonight.

Watching as the chauffeur came up the steps to her brownstone, Noelle quickly tossed Derrick's file into her large, black carryall tote, thinking she could continue her search on the way to the restaurant. By the time he rang the doorbell, she had her shawl draped around her shoulders and was headed to the door.

She paused in front of a decorative mirror hanging in the front hall. Her dark hair was curled in ringlets that fell around her face. She wore a light touch of eye shadow and lipstick that was her usual style. She'd considered doing something different but decided against it. Strangely enough, her usual style was comfortable and gave her a self-confidence she knew she would desperately need tonight.

She opened the door. "Ms. Brown, my name is Don. I'm Mr. Brandt's driver. Did you need more time?"

"No, I'm ready." She stepped out on the porch and locked the door behind her.

A few moments later, when Don opened the back door of the car, a box of perfect black baccara and black magic roses was lying on the seat.

"With Mr. Brandt's compliments," Don said, gesturing to the box.

As Noelle climbed into the car and lifted the box of roses onto her lap, the sweet perfume drifted up to her nose. Unable to resist, she lifted them closer, inhaling the wonderful smell. Apparently, Derrick had seduction skills she knew nothing about.

One hour and thirty minutes later, the car pulled up to a cliff overlooking the ocean. Don came around and opened the door, and as Noelle stepped out, her breath caught at the beauty of the scenery. The sun was setting behind them, and the light cast a luminous glow on the surface of the water. It was an unseasonably warm day. She didn't even need her coat; just the wrap would do.

As she walked to the edge of the cliff, she noticed a stairway built into the side of the hill that led down to the beach. Glancing down at the scene below, Noelle was stunned by what she saw.

The man standing on the beach near a clean, white, glowing tent was straight out of her secret fantasies.

Derrick was dressed casually in tan slacks and a nicely fitted V-neck sweater.

A single, round table covered in a white table cloth sat several feet from the edge of the tide. Candles of various heights lit the table. The quiet setting was broken by the hustle and bustle farther down the beach, where a group of culinary professionals—from chefs to wait staff—moved around in preparation.

After one of the white-coated staff noticed her and pointed her out to the others, the busy catering team seemed to pick up speed. Apparently, they'd been waiting for her.

Derrick started toward her, and it was only then that she noticed the single red rose in his hand. Realizing she was still standing thunderstruck at the top of the stairs, Noelle started down to meet him, stepping carefully.

As she reached the bottom step, he stopped her. "Heels. I should've guessed."

"You didn't say we were dining on a beach in New Jersey!" she countered, trying not to let her eyes roam over his form. He was an exceptionally handsome man.

Now he looked like... *Have mercy!*

"You have two choices. I can carry you to the table." His bad-boy grin appeared. "And I don't mind at all, or...you can get rid of those." He pointed at her shoes.

"What am I supposed to wear on my feet?"

"It's a beach. What do you normally wear?"

"Flip-flops," she answered sarcastically.

"Or nothing," he countered in a seductive drawl, and Noelle knew he was no longer discussing footwear.

She hesitated. The man was too smooth.

"Tell you what. If it'll make you feel better..." He lifted each of his feet and quickly snatched off his sandals. Tossing them away, he held out his arms. "See? Now we're even."

Noelle couldn't help the smile that came to her lips, understanding she was truly in something deeper and more dangerous than she'd first anticipated. Despite his personality flaws, and they were considerable, apparently her physical desire for him was stronger than she'd first suspected.

In public venues such as restaurants or the professional setting of her office, she was able to hold the intense attraction on a tight leash—barely. In this setting...she was not so certain she could.

But there was something different about Derrick tonight. There was a calmness about him that she'd never seen before.

He was always so wired and charged up, his sexual hunger so blatantly obvious. Before, she could recognize and deflect his advances with a sort of knowing ease because there was no doubt as to where they stood with each other. Yet tonight, his green eyes were the color of new spring leaves, and the fire that usually infused his every motion seemed somehow…suppressed.

This Derrick Brandt was far more dangerous than the other. Noelle knew without a doubt that if he kept up this gentle negotiation, she'd be removing more than her shoes tonight. That's what this whole seduction was about. A continuation of what had started in her office, the culmination of what had happened in the back of the restaurant.

Derrick Brandt had found a way around her defenses; something her life was desperately lacking…romance.

As much as she wanted to, she couldn't allow it. Noelle understood herself well enough to know that Derrick Brandt would eventually break her heart. His track record with women confirmed it.

"Well?" He watched her intently, almost daring her to choose option number one.

"Fine." She slipped her feet out of her heels; instead of tossing them away, she gently placed them together on the bottom step. "There, you happy?"

Taking her hand, he lifted it to her lips. "No, not yet. But I have a feeling you're the key."

What was that supposed to mean? She frowned. "This is just dinner and conversation, right?"

He started to lead her toward the table. "Right."

"I *won't* sleep with you."

"No, not tonight."

She stopped. "Not tonight. Not tomorrow night. Not any night. Dinner and conversation. And then we go back to matchmaker and client. That's the agreement, right?"

"Yes, that's the agreement. Three dates of my time

and choosing, interspersed with your attempts to pawn
me off on some other poor woman." He turned to face
her. "I'm not concerned with any of that right now.
Just tonight. And for the night, you're mine, and I
intend to make the most of it." His eyes sparkled with
sinful promise.

Lord, help me to keep my clothes on tonight. Noelle
said the quick prayer even as he took her hand again and
started toward the table.

"As far as what happens tomorrow," Derrick continued,
oblivious to her silent pleas, "I'll leave that up to you."

Almost an hour later, as the pair sat across from each
other sipping on the remnants of their wine, candles
were all around them. Derrick had spared no expense.
The tent was even heated. Derrick was forced to admit
that Camille could be on to something with this whole
kinder, gentler thing.

By allowing Noelle to set the pace of the evening,
he'd coaxed her out of her shell. She was relaxed where
she was normally on guard. Playful and witty where she
was stiff and snappy; flirtatious and tipsy where she was
normally resistant to the passion they brought out in one
another. It was a different side to her, and he was finding
he liked them both.

This woman was a drastic change from the one he'd
held in his arms a few days ago. Although she'd been as
hot for him as he was for her, as soon as the reality of what
was happening between them had settled in, it was clear
she instantly regretted it and became distant and defensive.

Now she was openly flirting. He was certain the few
glasses of wine she'd had had helped release her inhi-
bitions considerably. He was equally certain the other

Noelle—the staunchly professional Noelle—would regret her indulgence tomorrow.

Tipsy or sober, she was sexy as hell. And he was working hard to be Mr. Nice Guy when the beast in his soul was demanding he claim her. Right there on the beach before God, nature and man. He shifted in his chair, trying to find a position that did not further aggravate the ache in his crotch.

"You have the prettiest eyes, have I told you that?" She was grinning widely, and for the first time, Derrick noticed her dimpled cheeks.

"No," he answered, "but thank you. Yours are lovely."

"Oh, but not like yours." She shook her head, and it kind of wobbled.

Not for the first time, Derrick wondered if he should've cut her off sooner.

"No, yours are so…revealing. They tell everything you're thinking. You'd suck at poker."

Derrick frowned thoughtfully, knowing it was true.

"Like the speed dating mixer thing, every time the bell rang, you looked at me." She took another sip from the wineglass. "Know what I saw when you looked at me?"

His eyes shot to hers. "What?"

She giggled, and the sweet sound brought a smile to his face. "The same thing I see now! Sweaty sheets." She giggled and took another sip. "You. Me. And sweaty sheets." She waggled a finger at him. "You were thinking about sweaty sheets long before we went into the kitchen."

"You're right. I was."

Her pretty face sobered for a moment. She leaned across the table and her perfume drifted to his nose. "Pssst, can I tell you something?"

Derrick was unable to stop the smirk that came to his lips. This adorable whispering woman was so different from the dignified woman he'd met a few weeks ago.

"You can tell me anything."

"I was thinking about sweaty sheets, too."

Her heated response to his touch, as he held her propped against the sink that night left no questions about their agreement, but still, he said, "Really?"

"Oh, yeah." She giggled. "Ooh, yeah." She turned the glass up and swallowed the remaining wine. "Hey, where did the bottle go?" She frowned down at the candle-lit table. "It was just here a minute ago."

"I asked the waiter to take it and everything else away. The bottle was almost empty."

"Oh, well…" She rested her elbows on the table and leaned forward, bracing her chin on the heels of her hands. "Dinner was terrific. I'm glad we did this."

The motion pushed her full breasts together provocatively, and Derrick was instantly reminded of how she'd looked leaning against the kitchen sink of the restaurant. Her head thrown back in surrender, the welcoming moans of a woman on the edge of release. Holding the slight weight of each breast in his palms. The sweet taste of her on his tongue, the texture of her taut nipples, the feel of his coarse palm against her silky thigh, and the heat radiating from her center. Derrick felt his erection growing stronger.

"So am I." He knew they would have to cut the evening short. As much as he was enjoying himself, he couldn't keep up with this. He knew his nature well enough to understand that he was not about to make love to a intoxicated woman.

Derrick glanced down the beach to where the catering staff was packing their van in preparation to leave. "It's getting late. I better get you home."

Her eyes twinkled in the moonlight. "Whose home?"

He pushed away from the table. "It's definitely time to go. Come on." He walked around to her side of the table and pulled her chair back.

"What a gentleman," she giggled and stood with surprising grace. "You know, when you first came to my office, I thought you were a jackass."

"I know." He led her across the uneven sandy beach, bracing her weight against his side. Trying to ignore the wonderful feeling of her soft body pressed against his.

"It just didn't make any sense." She frowned. "You were so good-looking and such a jackass." She swung around to face him. "Why'd you have to be such a jackass?"

"It's just my nature, I suppose." He guided her to the bottom stair. "Watch your step."

She bent to pick up her heels and stood suddenly. "Whoa." She pulled away from him and braced her back against the banister. "I feel…funny." She rubbed her stomach.

"Oh hell." Derrick muttered.

She slumped down on the second stair and groaned. "I don't feel good."

Derrick glanced at Don waiting patiently at the top of the stairway, wondering if he should just give her a few minutes and see if nature took its course or try to get her up the steps to the car.

Derrick reached forward to push a few ringlets back off her face. He glanced down the beach, wondering if the catering people had something for an upset stomach, but their van was pulling away. "Damn."

He reached forward, lifting her under her knees and back. Cradling her in his arms, he started up the stairs.

"What are you doing?" she whined. "You can't carry me. I'm big!" She looked around nervously. "Derrick, we'll both fall and then…"

Derrick continued to climb the stairs. "Shh, and stop squirming."

"Derrick, put me… Oh, I feel…dizzy." She finally surrendered, wrapping her arms around his neck and resting her head against his chest.

Derrick reached the top of the stairs, and Don came forward to meet them. "Everything all right, sir?"

"Yes, although it appears Ms. Brown is a bit of a lightweight. One of her shoes, and my sandals are down on the beach. Can you run down and grab 'em?"

"Yes, sir." Trying to hide a small smile, Don darted down the stairs.

Derrick carried Noelle to the car and maneuvered to open the door. He started to place her gently on the seat but could not resist one tender kiss on her forehead.

The evening had not gone exactly as he'd planned, but aside from the possibility of her getting sick in his car, it hadn't turned out so badly. He'd gotten a chance to see the Noelle Brown he was sure not many people even knew existed. He gently sat her on the backseat and scooted her across before climbing in beside her.

She lay with her head back against the seat.

"Derrick…"she moaned plaintively. "Derrick, it hurts."

Is she for real? Derrick frowned, concerned for the first time. He pulled her against his side and pressed his palm against her mid section. "Where does it hurt?"

"Right here," she moaned, pushing his hand hard

against her lower stomach. She curled against his side. "Yeah, right there."

Derrick leaned back to look into her face. Something about her complaint didn't feel like a complaint. "What does it feel like?"

With a smile on her face, she pressed his hand harder against her stomach. "I ache." She guided his large hand lower.

Derrick finally understood. "Uh-uh." He yanked his hand away. "No, baby, there's nothing I can do about *that* ache. At least, not tonight." He kissed her forehead again and said a silent prayer for strength.

Feeling desperate, he glanced out the front window. "What the hell is taking Don so long?"

"Please, Derrick." In the absence of his hand, she pressed her own against her midsection. "Help me."

Derrick frowned at the small hand as it moved lower. If she only knew how desperately he wanted to *help her*. His eyes widened, as she suddenly began pulling at the buttons that lined the front of her slacks.

He covered her hands. "No, baby, please don't do this to me." He pleaded with her, but Noelle was so lost in her own world she ignored his words, as her right hand slipped inside her slacks.

Her thighs fell apart, and Derrick watched in stunned stillness as her small hand moved beneath the soft fabric working its way to the place he most wanted to be.

"I need…I need…" Her breathy cries were nothing less than pure torture.

He lay his head back against the seat and closed his eyes tightly, his throbbing erection straining painfully against his pant zipper. Derrick considered himself a strong man, but this provocative display was too much to ask.

His whole body stiffened feeling her soft touch on his arm.

"Derrick, please…"

Her short nails dug into the fabric of his sweater, and Derrick's eyes opened and focused on her face. He knew she'd found her center without ever lowering his eyes. The look of intense concentration as she bit into her bottom lip, her lush lashes lying against her cheek. He knew this is what she would look like in the throes of passion, with him buried deep inside her. And he knew if he did not take her eventually, this image would haunt him for a lifetime. *God, she's beautiful.*

Unable to stop himself, his eyes fell to the open flap of her pants, and the busy hand sliding back and forth beneath the fabric.

"Oh, Derrick! Oh, oh…" Her head tossed back and forth against the leather seat as she climbed to the mountaintop without him.

Damn. Derrick angrily balled his fist, resisting the urge to touch her, knowing if he did, he wouldn't stop. His own emotions spinning somewhere between intense arousal and anger, he sat spellbound watching her erotic behavior, unable to stop the images racing through his mind. Like the one of pulling her across his lap, spreading her open and plunging into her wet heat. Or laying her down on the seat and covering her body with his. Yes, it would be very easy to stop her ache, and his own. Tomorrow when she sobered up, how would she feel?

She was such a passionate woman, drunk or sober, but Derrick was determined that when they finally did make love—and that was now inescapable—Noelle would be fully aware of what she was doing. He would leave no room for regret or remorse.

Suddenly, the sharp nails dug deeper as she climaxed, crying out in release, and Derrick was almost ashamedly certain he'd come in his pants.

The slow moving hand slowed and finally stopped, and Derrick realized she'd fallen asleep. He lay his head back against the seat and let out a deep sigh of relief. "Just like a damn cat," he muttered with a shake of his head.

Just then, Don opened the front door and climbed in. "I found the shoe, sir."

"Great, now get us back to town—fast."

Don glanced at the pair through the rearview mirror and apparently saw too much. "Your town house, sir?"

"No." he returned the driver's stare until the other man looked away. "Ms. Brown's brownstone first."

"Yes, sir." The car began backing away from the cliff.

Derrick glanced over at his sleeping passenger once more, remembering what he'd just witnessed. She was sleeping soundly, having no idea of what she'd just put him through. Feeling a little more sure of his control now, he leaned forward and placed a light kiss on her soft lips.

"Don, can you recommend anything for a hangover?"

Don's smiling face appeared in the rearview mirror. "As a matter of fact, I have a guaranteed cure."

Derrick nodded, wondering if his ever-resourceful driver had anything for a never-ending hard-on. He chuckled to himself, realizing the cure for that was currently cuddled against his arm. "Soon, beauty… very soon."

Chapter 11

Over an hour later, as they entered the edge of town, Derrick started fishing around in the bottom of Noelle's large carryall bag, looking for her house keys. His hand wrapped around a large file folder, and when he pushed it to the side to continue his search, he noticed the name scribbled in elegant handwriting on the front of the file. He turned on the interior light. It was his.

Surprised, Derrick pulled the file from the bag and opened it. It was his case file. Apparently, Noelle had done a little homework.

Newspaper clippings and photos from public events were mixed with observations from their few meetings and the various efforts she'd made to find a match for him. What caught his attention the most were the notes she'd scribbled on the inside file jacket. They were dated with the date of their first meeting in her office.

Derrick Brandt on first impression is cold and calculating. Despite his physical attractiveness, there is an innate harshness about him that does not engage well. He appears to want a woman that is everything he is not. Warm, kind, concerned about his well-being, when it is apparent he has no intention of returning that regard.

What's most disappointing is that with some minor modifications, such as the development of a heart, he would really be quite a catch.

Derrick frowned down at the notes, taken aback by the words. It was amazing to believe that they'd come from the woman beside him. The one who'd been writhing and moaning against his side just a few minutes ago. Then again, that had been their first meeting.

He flipped to the next page of notes, dated a week prior:

Although Derrick Brandt appears to have all the resources imaginable at his disposal, the one thing he seems to lack in great quantity is empathy. It is this lack of empathy that causes him to be brutal in his remarks to women and impatient with the process of finding an appropriate match. He speaks when he should listen and has an alarming lack of understanding about the need for discretion and gentleness.

Despite the very large retainer we were given, I find it very unlikely that I will be able to find a suitable candidate for him. He may very well be my first failure.

Is that how you see me? he thought, glancing down at her softly snoring form. *Cold, calculating and lacking in empathy? A failure?*

Derrick returned the folder to her bag and finally found the house keys in the bottom. He spent the rest of the trip contemplating what he'd just read. And he'd tried so hard on this date to be compassionate and calm, just as Camille had advised.

Derrick had always known he lacked something, but he'd never been able to put his finger on it. Could it be empathy? That integral understanding of another man or woman's feelings and point of view.

He considered the people closest to him and knew that there was only one person that actually qualified: Camille. And she was well aware of his lack of discretion and gentleness.

Was that part of the problem? That his closest companion had no expectation of better behavior from him and therefore he gave none?

Noelle was waiting for something different. A man who did not chase her around tables. He shuddered, remembering her chastening him about his lack of dignity.

A few minutes later, they pulled up in front of her brownstone and Derrick carried her up the front steps and handed the key off to Don to unlock the door. He cradled his bundle close and watched the adjoining brownstones and across the street for voyeurs.

Once Don got the door open, Derrick carried her across the threshold. "Take a look in the kitchen and see if you can find the ingredients to whip up some of that hangover concoction you were telling me about a while back," Derrick, said heading down the hallway he assumed would lead to a bedroom.

"Um, sir, are you sure Ms. Brown would be okay with me in her kitchen?"

Derrick stopped short, as a chill ran down his spine. He was suddenly confronted with the truth of what Noelle had written in that file. It had not even occurred to him to consider how Noelle might feel with a man she did not know digging around in her kitchen. His only thought, his only concern, had been finding something for the monstrous headache he suspected she would wake up with.

Derrick glared at the other man, who apparently was in no shortage of that precious commodity called empathy. Apparently the instinct came naturally to Don.

"Sir, did I say something to offend you?" Don asked.

Derrick blinked to force away the intense scrutiny. It wasn't Don's fault he understood what Derrick did not.

"No, go on. I'll explain to Noelle that I gave you permission." Derrick was pretty certain that authorization wouldn't carry a feather with Noelle, but it was enough to get Don moving again.

Derrick only wanted her to not suffer unduly for her overindulgence with him. He wanted the overall memory of their date to be a good one.

As he maneuvered down the hall, he couldn't help but take in the tasteful decorations lining the walls. The colors consisting of yellows, oranges and rust-reds were unusual, but so was Noelle Brown.

He finally found her bedroom at the end of the hall and gently laid her across the bed. Standing beside the bed, Derrick tried to will his feet to move, but she was so beautiful lying there with her arms over her head, her long body stretched out before him.

Cold, calculating and lacking in empathy. Overall, it

wasn't the worst description he'd ever received. But somehow the words stung worse than any he remembered.

Maybe because of the dispassionate way in which the conclusions had been drawn. Maybe it was the knowledge that even as she moved against his body in sexual need, she considered him *without a heart*. Or maybe it was because he'd never truly cared what anyone thought of him before. Until now.

True, he wanted her body, he wanted to hold her through the night and wake beside her in the morning. More importantly, he wanted Noelle's respect and regard. He wanted her to think well of him. He wanted her to want him. *Really* want him. The way he wanted her. Every part of her.

He rubbed his chin thoughtfully, suddenly feeling like the Tin Man in *The Wizard of Oz*. That is, if the Tin Man had it bad for Dorothy. With a shake of his head, he bent and place a gentle kiss on her forehead.

"One day soon, sweetheart." He promised with a whisper. "One way or another, I'm going to find a way to make you want me."

She stirred, rolling to her side. Derrick felt the throbbing in his slacks once again and knew it was time to go. A few seconds later, he found Don in the kitchen mixing up a batch of what he called *Morning After*.

A few minutes later, the two men locked the door from the inside and let themselves out.

"I want to die…." Noelle turned over in her bed, holding her pounding head between her hands. She rolled to the edge of the bed and attempted to stand, but the floor wouldn't cooperate by standing still, so she curled back up in a ball.

As she lay there, vague recollections of the night before started to come back to her. The candlelit table on the beach, the beautiful sunset over the ocean, the wonderful meal, her overindulgence in wine, and, finally, the reason for her overindulgence in wine.

Derrick Brandt's seduction…and the news that really got her: her sister leaving town.

Sometime during the main course of their dinner, Noelle had come to the realization that Derrick was not just a man—he was some type of unknown chameleon.

Over the evening, he'd transformed right before her eyes. He'd stopped being the difficult, blunt jackass she'd come to know and started channeling the spirit of Casanova. He was charming, interesting and the most shocking of all—funny. And slowly, minute by minute, she felt herself becoming defenseless.

Despite all that, she knew it was not the reason for her aching head this morning. No, this was a downfall of her own making. She'd made the mistake of asking Derrick about his childhood. Like most Philadelphians, she knew only snippets of his rags-to-riches story as told by what the tabloids could dig up. The truth, the painful truth, was something that could only be told by the man.

She'd asked, and for whatever reason, he'd decided to tell her. His whole long, heartbreaking story. Of his years in foster homes, and how he'd come to be there, right up until the day he found Camille Massey.

He'd told her all about Royce Massey and what the man had come to represent to him, and then…he'd looked at her with those beautiful eyes, and for the first time, there was no sexual desire or calculation reflected there, just…a need to be understood, and sadness.

A sadness so deep and intense, Noelle had to fight

an almost overwhelming need to circle the table and put her arms around him. With that one look, he invited her into his soul, and what she found there was not what she'd expected. Not a cocky, overbearing Neanderthal, but a troubled man who'd seen more than his fair share of disappointment in life. All the sweet, inviting words in the world could not have seduced her any better than that one single glance. Not knowing how else to comfort him and so sad he endured all that drama, she'd picked up her wineglass that moment and, quite frankly, could not remember putting it down for the rest of the night.

Despite the throbbing headache, she struggled up to her elbows to look around, realizing that she was lying in her own bed. Fully dressed. That bed was a good sign. Or was it? She was more than certain her own two feet could not have brought her, which left only Derrick.

She fell back onto the bed and let complete humiliation wash over her. *What the hell is wrong with you?* she silently chided herself. *I've rarely gotten so tipsy before in my life!*

With a sigh, she decided to attempt to stand once more. Although the room still swayed slightly, she was able to work her way into the hall and along the corridor. As she approached the kitchen, she noticed her carryall bag sitting on a chair in the hall.

She paused, realizing Derrick had probably gone into her bag to get her keys. Had he seen the file? Did it matter? Not at the moment, she finally decided. Right now, all that mattered was making the room stop spinning.

She turned the corner and headed into the kitchen to get a glass of water for her parched throat. Turning on the faucet, she reached into the overhead cabinet and pulled down a glass. Just as she turned back to the sink, she noticed a note on the refrigerator door.

Left something in the fridge to help your hangover.

She opened the door. Sitting on the top shelf was a pitcher of something that resembled tomato sauce.

She lifted the pitcher to her nose. "Eeewww!" She sat it down abruptly on a nearby counter. "*That* is *nasty.*"

Just then, what sounded like the bells of Notre Dame began to rang, and she quickly covered her ears. Once the sound was muted, she was able to determine that it was only a ringing telephone.

She hurried to answer it, just to stop the noise. "Hello?" she whispered.

"Good morning," Derrick's clear, smooth voice responded, not sounding even the slightest bit hungover.

"If you say so." She braced her weight against the countertop.

"Did you find the elixir in the fridge?"

"Yes."

"Did you drink it?"

"No."

"Why not?"

"It smells gross."

"Drink it. Don swears by it."

"Don?"

"Yeah, my driver. You met him last night."

She covered her face, realizing she'd forgotten the other witness to her embarrassing behavior. "Oh, yeah."

"How do you feel?"

She sighed. "Like I got run over by a bus."

He laughed, and the deep sound reverberated through

the phone. "Yeah, you were really putting it away last night."

Noelle was extremely grateful that he was on the other end of the phone and therefore could not see her mortification. Not knowing what she could say in her defense, since the truth was totally unacceptable, she chose to say nothing.

"Well, just wanted to make sure you were up and going this morning," he continued. "And drink that elixir. You'll feel better by noon."

"All right—and thanks for getting me home safely."

"My pleasure," he purred.

The sensual quality in his voice made Noelle look down at her pantsuit once again. She quickly ran her hand over the zipper at the back of her sequined top to be sure it was still in place. He sounded too much like a satisfied male to have gone home empty-handed.

"Um, Derrick…did we?"

"I promise, sweetness, if we did, you'd remember."

"Hmm."

"Don't worry, your virtue is still intact for now."

"For now?"

"Just drink the elixir and get to work. You still have to find a date for me, remember?"

That final statement felt like a blow to her midsection. "You've changed your mind about our agreement?" *About wanting me?*

"Not even close. But this was the deal. One date with you, one date with a potential match, right?"

"Yes, that's the deal. Thank you for keeping up your part of it."

"Oh, I'll fulfill my part of the bargain. Question is, will you?"

"What's that supposed to mean?"

"Nothing. Just drink that elixir. Otherwise you'll end up nursing a headache all day."

"Okay, and, Derrick, thanks again."

"No, thank you, Noelle. You gave me a night to remember and one I will always cherish." With that, he hung up.

A night to remember? Noelle frowned at the phone and unconsciously touched her zipper once more. She had no idea what that comment meant, but regardless, she still had a business to run.

Noelle turned to the mixture sitting on the counter. She lifted the pitcher, and the pungent odor drifted into her nose once more.

"Ugh, this is some nasty stuff." She shook her body slightly, in an attempt to build her nerve. "You better be right about this, Don the driver." And quickly, before she could change her mind, she turned the pitcher bottoms up.

Chapter 12

As Derrick bit into another forkful of cauliflower, he glanced at the woman sitting across from him. "Veterinarian. That's interesting."

She smiled, and Derrick was struck again by Noelle's instinctive understanding of him. Belinda Foster appeared to be everything he'd hoped to find the day he walked into Love Unlimited. She was bright, articulate, wanted a large family and a quiet life. And despite all that, Derrick could not muster even a fraction of enthusiasm for her.

The why was no great mystery. It simply came down to two words. *Want* and *need*. Derrick had gone to Love Unlimited looking for what he thought he needed and instead had found what he truly wanted.

"Have you always been artistic?" Belinda was asking as she toyed with her potatoes, her brown eyes watching him shyly. She was the polar opposite of the women he'd previously dated.

The women he'd chosen for himself were all wrong, chosen randomly and without much thought beyond sexual gratification. Those women were gorgeous, whereas Belinda was mildly pretty. But there was another quality about her; sweetness. She was shy and slightly timid, whereas he was normally paired with tigresses. She was successful in her own right, whereas he was usually left carrying the financial load. And she wanted nothing more than a big family. She was just what he'd asked Noelle to find. And now, he didn't want her.

What he wanted was the prickly passion that was unique to Noelle, both tigress and kitten, bold and shy, and a beauty that was all her own. He didn't really know where she stood on the whole family issue, but somehow that wasn't the deal breaker it once was.

Now all that mattered was changing Noelle's opinion of him. And unfortunately, that meant accepting this ridiculous arrangement of alternately dating her and clients of hers he had no interest in. Granted, not the most traditional way to woo a woman, but at this point his options were limited. Derrick had learned years ago in bidding on various projects that sometimes the best way to obtain what you wanted was to give something in return.

"No, actually. I only developed an interest in my teens," he answered, and discreetly glanced at his watch.

"Did you grow up here in Philly?" she asked casually.

Derrick glanced at her, wondering if she were asking questions to which she already knew the answers just to make conversation. Thanks to the tabloids, most of his background was public knowledge. "Um, yes. Yourself?"

She smiled again and Derrick was convinced the

question had been as innocent as it sounded. "Born and bred."

The conversation continued in the same pleasant though stilted and surface-y pattern before Derrick finally took her home.

As he walked her to the door, she slowed her pace. "Do you want to come in for some coffee?"

He smiled politely. "Not tonight, but I did have a good time."

Her eyebrows crinkled in confusion as she eased a little closer. "It's okay, you know…I mean, if you want to."

Derrick was slightly taken aback by the blatant offer. "Um, I'm flattered, but maybe we should take things slow."

"You're right. It's just, I really like you, Derrick, and I think this is the beginning of something special. Don't you?"

Derrick, not knowing what to say in response, placed a gentle kiss on her cheek. "Good-night." Without waiting for a response, he turned and started back down the walkway to his car.

Noelle glanced at the clock on her nightstand for the twentieth time. It read ten fifty-three. She pounded her pillow and changed position once more.

She was certain Derrick's date with Belinda was probably going well. Belinda was everything he said he wanted in a woman. She'd made sure of that. Certain that the sooner she could satisfy his requirements, the sooner she could get rid of him.

And she had to get rid of him.

Yes, there was no doubt, they were probably enjoying a nice, cozy dinner. She couldn't help wondering what kind of date he'd planned, given his unexpected romantic streak. Never in a million years would she have imagined him to be the romantic-candlelit-dinner-on-the-beach type. But he was. In truth…he was probably the most romantic man she'd ever met.

She glanced over her shoulder at the clock once more. Ten fifty-five. She flipped over onto her back and stared up into the darkness. *What is wrong with me?*

"I do not want Derrick Brandt." She chanted aloud. "I do not want Derrick Brandt."

She turned onto her side once more, wondering when exactly this had happened. What was the precise moment she had started falling for him? There was no point denying it any longer.

The man was an obnoxious, arrogant, unfeeling jerk. And she would give anything to have him beside her at this very moment.

The thought made her heart skip a terrified beat as it brought to mind another possibility. What if his date with Belinda went *extremely* well? What if, right now, he was with her…making love?

"Not my concern," she muttered, trying desperately to convince herself of that. "He would've only hurt me, eventually. He's not capable of the kind of relationship I need. Belinda's better for him."

The shrill ringing of the phone startled her. She glanced at the clock—ten fifty-eight—before grabbing the cordless off her night stand. "Hello?"

"Good, you're still awake." Derrick's deep voice flowed over her aching heart like a mystical ointment. "Just wanted to tell you, Belinda's nice, but it's not going to work out. Keep looking."

Noelle fought back the urge to grin. "Sorry to hear that. Can I ask why?"

"Just chalk it up to chemistry."

Something occurred to Noelle. "Why are you calling me at home? You could've called the office and told me this tomorrow."

"Do you mind?"

"No." Noelle waited for him to say something more, but several seconds passed in silence before Noelle began to think maybe the call had dropped. "Derrick?"

"Yeah, I'm here."

"Well, okay, I'll pick out some more profiles tomorrow, and give you a ca—"

"Why are you still awake?" he asked. His voice was gruff with some emotion she did not recognize.

"Can't sleep."

"Can I come over?"

"What?"

"Nothing—never mind. Just call me with the new profiles."

This time when the line went silent, there was no question that he'd hung up.

Noelle replaced the phone on the base and pushed herself into a sitting position. *Can I come over?* That's what he'd said. *Can I come over?*

Noelle replayed the conversation in her head with various answers.

Can I come over? Of course not! What kind of woman do you think I am?

Can I come over? Yes—and hurry!

She climbed out of the bed, wandered into the kitchen and turned on the light. Her mind was still racing with the implications of those four little words. If he'd lost interest in her, would he want to come over at eleven o'clock at night?

Reaching overhead, she took a glass from the cabinet. Taking the juice bottle from the fridge, she poured half a cup and put it back.

She leaned back against the counter and smiled to herself. He still wanted her.

She finished her juice and placed the cup in the dishwasher. Turning off the light, she headed back to her bedroom still not the slightest bit sleepy.

At least she took comfort in knowing she was not the only one sleeping alone tonight.

Chapter 13

"I'm going to miss you so much." Noelle slowly wrapped a ceramic statue in newspaper. "Who am I going to talk to about my man troubles?"

Kimber stood straight from where she was bent unhooking her cable box. "What man troubles?"

"I'm just saying."

"Exactly." Kimber turned in her direction, her hand on her hip. "You never say. So, what man troubles are you having?"

"No man troubles. I'm just saying for future reference."

Kimber's eyes narrowed on her face. "Hmm." She returned to unhooking wires. "I love you, Noelle, but it's not like you've ever really confided your secrets in me."

"I knew you were here if I ever wanted to. No one in the family has ever moved away before."

"First time for everything. Can you drop this box off

at the cable office for me? Not sure I'll have time this weekend." She removed the cable box from the entertainment center and placed it on the end of the sofa.

"Yeah. What do you mean, I never confided in you? We talk."

"Yeah, but we don't talk-talk." She glanced around the crowded room, full of half-packed boxes and shipping materials. "You know, like girlfriends."

Noelle found herself deeply hurt by the comment. Maybe her sister wasn't as heartbroken by this move as she herself was. "I always thought we were close."

"We are." She turned to face Noelle. "Just not like that. Don't look at me like that. I didn't mean anything bad by it. It's just some sisters are really tight, and some are just…sisters."

"We're just sisters?"

"Yeah, but it's cool. Oh, come on! Why are you crying?"

Noelle hastily wiped at her tear-filled eyes. "Never mind."

Kimber flopped down on the floor and crossed her legs. "Okay, what gives?"

"You're moving across the country and leaving your family, and you don't care. You don't care!" Unable to hold back any longer, the tears flowed. "It's like I'm the only one who thinks there is something wrong with all this!"

Kimber sat staring with her arms propped on her knees while Noelle poured out two weeks' worth of misery. When she was all cried out, she finally collapsed on the sofa.

"Wow, that was something."

Noelle glared at her sister. "You can be a real bitch."

Kimber grinned. "See…the fact that you are *just now* realizing that only confirms my point." She reached over and grabbed a roll of paper towels and handed it to Noelle. "Okay, this is not about my move. What's going on with you?"

Noelle ripped off a couple of paper towels and wiped her face. "I don't know."

"Humph, I guess it's about time. Me and Ray had bets on when you would blow."

"What?"

"Well, you're always wound so tight, it had to happen." She leaned back on one of the large boxes sitting in the middle of the floor. "I wonder… Something had to set this off, and I don't think it's my move. So, what's going on?"

Noelle glanced at her sister. Much as she hated to admit it, Kimber was right. Despite the closeness of their family, she'd never taken to really truly confiding in anyone. She needed to talk to someone about this or she really would explode.

"I think I'm falling in love with one of my clients."

Kimber sat straight up. "Whoa. Really? Who?"

"Derrick Brandt."

"The architect? He's a client of yours?"

"Yes. For about a month now."

"A month? And you're already falling for him? Are you getting busy with this guy?"

"No! Of course not!"

"Hey, don't get indignant with me." Kimber wagged a finger at her. "You're the one talking about falling for a guy you've known a month. So naturally the first thing that comes to my mind is really good, head-banging sex."

Noelle smirked. "I think I remember why I've never confided in you before."

"Sorry, I couldn't resist. You're usually so…"

Noelle was instantly reminded of her brother's similar statement and felt her temper flare. "Usually so what? Goody-goody?"

"Well…yeah."

"What does that mean anyway?"

"Hold up, why are you getting so angry with me? I'm just trying to help."

"Oh, never mind. I'm sorry I said anything. Let's just get this finished so I can go home."

Kimber's smile fell away. "I'm sorry. It's obvious you are really struggling with this thing, and that was totally insensitive of me." She got up off floor and sat down next to Noelle on the sofa. "Okay, let's start over. Tell me about the architect."

The sincerity in her sister's eyes gave Noelle the courage to go forward. "He's gorgeous, he's brilliant and he's a complete jackass."

Kimber chuckled knowingly.

Something about the laugh caught Noelle's attention. "What was that laugh about?"

"He sounds like my kind of guy."

"Well, you can't have him."

Kimber laughed outright. "Don't worry, I wouldn't dare come between you and the first sign of a love life you've shown in, what, three years?"

Noelle pursed her lips in embarrassment. "Two and a half."

"Oh yeah, that speed-reader guy, right?"

"He was a fact-checker."

"Yeah, I remember." Kimber shook her head. "He was as stiff as you. You guys were like some kind of Stepford couple. Ray couldn't stand him, by the way."

"Really?"

She nodded.

"Well, Derrick is nothing like him. In fact, just the opposite."

"Hmm. Okay, let me consider what that means. Since you are in complete control of your every action like some kind of robot—today's behavior notwithstanding—that must mean he's an emotional mess. Which would make sense, given the things I've read about him."

Noelle frowned. "Don't believe everything you've read. Though he does say things without the slightest bit of forethought."

"So." Kimber placed her arm around her sister's shoulders. "Tell me about him."

"There's something there that I can't quite put my finger on." Noelle glanced at her. "I feel like he *needs* me. But he's so brutal in some ways, I'm afraid he'll hurt my feelings. Not to mention my heart."

"Have you told him how you feel?"

"No. At least, I don't think so."

"You don't think so?"

"Um, yeah." Noelle slid away. "We went out together a few nights ago, and I may have had a little too much to drink. I can't seem to remember everything that happened."

Kimber's laugh was absolutely joyful. "Oh, my God! You got drunk! You! Oh, I can't wait to tell Ray!" She jumped to her feet, looking in every direction. "Where's that dang phone?"

"You better not!"

Kimber continued to push stuff around, seeking the phone.

"Kimber! Please, I need to talk to someone about this, and if not you…" The tears burst forth again.

In a flash, her sister was beside her, pulling her into her arms. "Shh, I'm sorry. Wow, once you get started… Shh, it's okay. I'm sorry. I'll shut up and listen now."

For several minutes the sisters just sat cuddled together, Kimber gently rocking them back and forth.

Finally, Kimber's soft voice broke the silence. "I think you need to have a long heart-to-heart with this guy, and both of you need to get everything out in the open. You're obviously torn over what you feel. I'm not sure about him, but if he's nearly as confused as you…"

"Yeah, I know. I'm just so afraid he could hurt me."

"Noelle, pain is a part of life. You can't get around it. You just have to decide what is and is not worth the hurt." She sat up and turned Noelle to face her. "Remember, D'Andre? That guitarist I dated a few months back?"

"A little. The one with the Mohawk?" Noelle wiped her eyes with her crumpled paper towel.

"Yeah, that's him. I thought I was absolutely in love with that man. Let's just say he had a habit of letting the head between his legs off its leash. I would go to hear him play, and there would be all these women waiting backstage for him, and it wasn't like they didn't know he had a girlfriend. They just didn't care. Every time I confronted him, he promised it would never happen again. We both knew he was lying." She leaned back against the sofa cushions. "I was so unhappy, and finally I decided that what I was getting out of the relationship was not worth what I was putting into it. I had to give him up, and overall I don't really regret it, but some days I wonder if he would have eventually grown up. Could we have made it? That's a doubt I have to live with. I made a choice. That's what you have to do. Just lay it all on the line with this guy, and then…make a choice."

"It's not that simple."

"Why not?"

"It just isn't." She stood. "Thank you for listening to me bawl like a baby." She forced a smile. "I do appreciate this, but the more I think about it, the more I realize that getting involved with Derrick Brandt is a bad idea. Let's finish this up and get some lunch."

For several minutes, Kimber sat staring up at her sister. "You know, even though I'm moving, I'm only a phone call away. If you ever need to talk…"

This time Noelle's smile was sincere. "I know. Thanks." She glanced around the room. "Now, let's get you packed up. I'm suddenly in a hurry to get rid of you."

"Hey!" Kimber threw a pillow at her. "I think this whole sister-bonding thing is going quite well." Her face sobered. "I'm just sorry we took this long to open up to each other."

"Yeah, me, too."

The pair returned to their packing, and almost two hours later were close enough to finishing that they decided to take a break and run down to the Mickey D's on the corner from Kimber's apartment building.

Although she kept her contemplations to herself the rest of the morning, Noelle could not stop thinking about Derrick Brandt. *Can I come over?*

What if she'd said yes? How different would the world have seemed this morning? Would they have had time to discuss their conflicted feelings? Probably not, she decided. No, they would've been too busy making the sheets sweaty.

Sitting in the busy fast-food restaurant, Noelle finally resigned herself to the fact that if the idea of Derrick Brandt could cause her this much anguish, a real relationship would damn near drive her insane. No, it was best to leave matters as they stood. There was obviously no future for her and Derrick Brandt.

Across town, Derrick was sitting in a lounge chair in the quiet, soothing bedroom of Camille's estate home, where she received her daily physical therapy, while they discussed the next phase of their game plan.

"Define empathy," Derrick demanded, crossing his leg over his knee.

"What do you mean, define it? You know what empathy is. Putting yourself in someone else's place, trying to feel what they feel, see the world through their eyes and with their considerations. Why?" Camille responded from where she lay on the massage table.

"Apparently...I lack empathy," he grumbled. "She wrote it in my case file."

"Astute young woman."

"What's that supposed to mean?" Derrick looked away as the nurse finished the massage and wrapped a robe around Camille's shoulders.

After almost ten years of meeting this way, Derrick was now immune to the odd sensation of discussing business with a towel-clad older woman.

After the death of Royce, Camille had used the daily running of the firm to fill the void in her life. For a period of several years, she'd lived and breathed all aspects of Massey Architectural, and Derrick, understanding the pain that motivated her, and not knowing how else to help, had done everything to accommodate her. Including meeting at all times of the day or night and in just such situations.

Over the years, he'd learned a great deal about the inner workings of running a multimillion-dollar business. At the same time, he'd grown to love and respect Camille more, even as he came to realize that she was mentoring him to take her place as the head of the company. Over time, their discussions had grown and evolved to include everything from business strategies to more personal affairs of their lives.

"Well, considering she's only known you, what, a couple of weeks?" Camille tied the belt on her robe and turned to face him. "It took me almost a year to realize that."

"And why haven't you ever told me I was so easy to read?" Derrick glared, feeling slightly betrayed. "According to her, all it takes is one look in my eyes to know what I'm thinking."

Camille smiled. "She's discovered that, too, huh?" She headed in his direction to take a seat on the lounger beside him. "I think I like this young lady."

"Well?"

"Well, what?"

"Why haven't you ever told me these things. We're supposed to be business partners."

"Exactly when and how was I supposed to tell you that you lacked empathy, Derrick? During that first year as a co-op when you were so pitifully trying to find your place in the world? Or after Royce died and you were so vulnerable to any criticism?" She shrugged. "As for the other, why *would* I tell you you're easy to read? For years, that was my trump card and your only real redeeming quality. Telling you would've given you the advantage, and that wouldn't be very smart, would it?"

"And no one would dare call you stupid."

She smiled. "Thank you." She frowned. "I think."

"Okay, so now what?"

"Well, I was thinking that maybe she and I should spend some quality time together."

"Oh, no." He shook his head frantically. "Why? What purpose would that serve?"

"None—except to satisfy my curiosity." Camille's playful grin took twenty years off her age. "Consider it my payment for helping you."

Derrick glared at his friend and mentor. "Sounds more like blackmail than compensation."

She shrugged. "Well?"

"Just how do you propose we go about getting you two together?"

"Oh, Derrick." She shook her head. "Has twenty-five years with me taught you nothing?"

"Noelle, your three o'clock is here." Terri's eyes twinkled with suppressed humor that Noelle did not understand.

"Thank you, Terri, please show her in."

The door opened wider and an elegantly dressed elderly woman leaning heavily on a cane appeared in the door. Her vaguely familiar face was spread in a pleasant smile.

"Thank you, sweetheart." She smiled up at Terri before starting slowly across the room toward Noelle.

Noelle smiled as she came around the desk to greet her. "Ms. Massey? Noelle Brown, nice to meet you."

Camille searched the younger woman's eyes for any sign of recognition and found none. "Please call me Camille. You don't remember me, do you?"

She frowned. "We've met?"

"At Dmitri's. I was with Derrick Brandt." She settled into one of the guest chairs.

Noelle's eyes widened in recognition. "Oh, yes, now I remember." She took her seat behind the desk. "His business partner, right?"

Camille watched the woman's demeanor change. Where she had just been welcoming, she suddenly became guarded.

"I understand you're looking for a companion for shows and dinner." She glanced down at the notes in her file. "A mature man with a worldly sense of style who enjoys cultural entertainment."

Camille nodded. "Yes. You know, Derrick recommended your agency."

"Really?" She scribbled something in the file. "Then he may have explained how it works." She reached into a drawer and pulled out a brochure, laying it open before her.

Camille frowned down at the smiling-faced couples and considered how to get this meeting back on track. Apparently, the matchmaker was determined to do her job, when the only reason Camille had made the appointment was to get a chance to talk to her about Derrick.

"Derrick was telling me how terrific you've been in his effort to find a lady friend."

"He did?" She pointed to the brochure. "As you can see, we offer a six-month guarantee. If we are not able to find someone compatible for you within six months, you get an additional six months of service free."

"Uh-huh. He was telling me that you yourself are single."

"Yes." She gave an artificial smile. "Unfortunately, I have not found my match yet, but I have successfully matched forty couples, twenty-nine of whom have gone on to marry."

"Derrick was telling me that—twenty-nine, really?"

She pointed to the brochure again. "Yes, in fact, here we have a few testimonials."

Reluctantly, Camille fished in her small handbag and pulled out her reading glasses to take a look at the brochure. "I knew you were doing well, but I did not realize you were so successful."

"Actually, all the couples we've matched are still together, only some of them have yet to marry. So we can really boast a one hundred percent compatibility rating."

"Hmm, that's very interesting."

Noelle paused in speaking and Camille looked up. "I must admit that I am a little surprised Mr. Brandt spoke so highly of our service. I had the impression he was not exactly happy with the service we'd provided him so far."

This was the opportunity she'd been waiting for, Camille thought. Noelle had initiated a discussion about Derrick, but to tell the truth the information in the brochure was becoming more interesting. "Yes, he's probably more impressed than you would think. So, how does this work?"

"Normally, we do a short interview and complete your application. During our phone call the other day, you were so precise in what you were looking for that I was able to get a fair impression, and I think I may have found a match for you."

Camille's eyes widened as she peered at the other woman over the top of her bifocals. "Really?"

Noelle smiled and nodded. "I have him on video if you're interested in seeing it."

Camille's mind was racing. She'd come here for

Derrick and somehow discovered that there could be a mature gentleman available to go around to shows and dinner with her. Camille had never revealed to Derrick just how lonely life had been these ten years without Royce.

She'd often thought it would be nice to have a gentleman friend. Someone around her age, with shared interests. It had just never occurred to her that she might be able to find him.

"Would you like to see the video?" Noelle was asking.

An hour later, Camille came out of Noelle's building and found a smiling Don standing by the curb and holding the car door open. Camille smiled back, feeling more buoyed and optimistic than she had in a long time.

Chapter 14

Derrick stood at the end of the walkway leading to the front door of the Brown family home. "Noelle, I'm not so sure about this."

I am, Noelle thought. One look in his eyes and she knew his hesitation was due to nerves, not annoyance.

"This was *your* idea," she taunted.

"Uh, no, it wasn't." He arched an eyebrow. "My idea was a relaxing candlelit dinner."

"And…I told you that tonight was not good. I had plans. How about tomorrow? And you said—"

"Yeah, yeah, I know what I said." He shook his head and started up the walk.

Noelle smiled and followed him. What he'd said was that he did not want to wait until tomorrow to have their second date. And after her heart-to-heart with Kimber, she'd had the inspiration to invite him to her family's traditional holiday dinner.

Normally, the family dinner was held on Christmas Eve, but with Kimber leaving for L.A., they'd pushed up the date.

Since their first date, Noelle had not been able to erase the images of a loveless childhood that he'd unknowingly given her. There had not been a trace of self-pity in his voice as he recounted his Christmases in foster homes. It was what was *not* said that had left the greatest impression.

There was no Santa Claus whose sole purpose in life was to bring happiness to kids and to give generously. There were no songs sung around a Christmas tree, no warm dinner with family gathered round, and no anticipating Christmas morning and what you would find under the tree.

She had no idea what would come of her relationship with Derrick Brandt, but one thing was for certain. Just this once, she could give him Christmas through the eyes of a child.

As they approached the porch, the door opened and Kimber and Ann appeared wearing matching expressions of curiosity and smiles.

Noelle knew what they were thinking. Her decision to bring Derrick had been so last minute that she had not had time to inform her family.

As they came up the steps, she made the introductions. "Derrick, this is my sister, Kimber, and my sister-in-law, Ann. Hey, guys, sorry I'm late."

As Derrick nodded in greeting, Ray came up behind Ann and, standing a foot taller than she, had a clear view of the unexpected guest.

"And this is my brother, Dr. Raymond Brown. Ray, Derrick Brandt."

Even before Derrick uttered a word, Noelle knew her brother was about to give her a reason to kill him.

With absolutely no consideration, Ray blurted out what the others were only thinking. "Noelle brought a man."

And he disappeared from the door. She knew he was rushing off to report this amazing development to her parents.

She glanced at Derrick to gauge his reaction and her admiration for the man grew a hundredfold as he pretended not to be surprised by her brother's outburst.

As grateful as she was, she knew they still had not run the gauntlet completely. As they entered the house, Noelle saw her mother coming from the kitchen, wiping her hands on a dish towel. To the left, her father was coming out of his study with Ray right behind him. Every pair of eyes was trained firmly on her and her guest.

Noelle decided there was nothing to be done except to simply rip the bandage off. "Everyone, this is Derrick Brandt. Derrick, my mother, Claudia, my father, Gil, and the Paul Revere imitator you met earlier, my brother, Ray. And you already met Ann and Kimber. Did I forget anyone?" she asked innocently, knowing the immediate response she would get.

Suddenly her sleeve was being pulled on. "Auntie, you forgot us!" Lea was staring up at her with a hard frown, and her sister, Lena, wore a matching expression.

She squatted down. "Oh, no!" She scooped them close and hugged them tight.

"How could I have forgotten the two prettiest girls in the whole world?" She turned to look up at Derrick. "Lea, Lena, I would like you to meet a friend of mine. This is Derrick."

She watched as Derrick's expression registered the

fact that he was looking at two identical faces. He nodded and said hello to the girls. Satisfied they had not been overlooked, they scampered off to continue shaking boxes under the tree.

Her mother had come forward and now extended a hand in welcome. "Welcome, Derrick, it's nice to meet you."

Derrick took the extended hand. As the others crowded in around them expressing the same sentiment, Noelle breathed a sigh of relief.

A couple of hours later, as they settled around the colorful Christmas tree that sat in one corner of the living room, Derrick watched the Brown family interact.

It was obvious they were a close-knit group. They joked and interacted with an ease Derrick could only imagine. Did he have siblings somewhere in the world? He knew little about his birth parents, his earliest memories being of the foster family he was living with when he started school. Thinking back, he couldn't even remember the reason they took him out of that first home.

Once he became a man, the resentfulness regarding his birth family was so deeply embedded that he had no desire to find them, and no need, because by then he had Camille. She was more of a mother to him that any he'd ever known.

Derrick watched the twin girls tearing into colorfully wrapped bags and boxes and soon realized this gathering was mostly for their benefit. Opening package after package containing everything from new dolls to clothes, they wore matching dimpled smiles that reminded him of Noelle.

He noticed the adults had only opened a few gifts themselves despite the number of large boxes under the tree. Seeing the question in his eyes, Noelle leaned toward him.

"We usually do this on Christmas Day, but with Kimber leaving for California, we decided to let the girls open some of their gifts early."

He looked into her soft, brown eyes, wondering if he would've ended up more like her had he been raised in this setting. Or was his personality preset? Would he have had more of that elusive empathy, that kindness and compassion she thought lacking in him had he been nurtured by loving parents from a young age?

"Here." A medium-size box was suddenly plopped on his lap. "It's a sweater." One of the twins—he still couldn't tell them apart—was staring up at him with big brown eyes.

The other twin toddled over to stand by her sister. "Open it," she said before beginning to tear at the paper herself. Apparently, he'd waited too long.

He watched as the two girls tore the red paper off the box and opened it to reveal a bright pink sweater. In the center was a laughing Santa with bells, sequins and tassels hanging from his button stitches.

One of the girls patted the sweater to make the bells jingle. "See?"

Derrick looked at the two sets of proud, bright eyes staring up at him, having no idea what to say. "Um…" He turned to find Noelle fighting to hide a grin, but she offered no help.

"Thank you?"

"It's not yours," the one on the left clarified with a slight frown.

"It's just so you have a gift, too," the other finished the thought.

"Oh." He glanced at Noelle for help again. She was still grinning, but no help was forthcoming. "Thanks again. It's…very nice. Thanks."

Their matching smiles appeared. Apparently, he'd given the right answer. Satisfied, the girls returned to playing with their own gifts.

Noelle leaned toward him and whispered, "I can't wait to see you in it." She laughed.

"You're going to be waiting a long time."

Just then, a bunch of commotion came from the back part of the house. A loud clanking bell, and stomping feet, and then, much to his amazement, Derrick heard a distinct booming voice shout out "Ho, ho, ho."

And then Santa appeared. Derrick noticed right away that the Santa beneath the red padded suit and white beard bore a striking resemblance to Gil Brown. He glanced around, wondering when the man had slipped out to prepare for this little production.

"Santa!" The twins both tried to scuttle to their feet at the same time. Using each other to stand, they inadvertently pulled each other down before finally getting to their feet and racing across the room to greet the visitor.

Santa scooped each up in an arm as the girls giggled loudly.

That was expected. What Derrick did not anticipate was the reaction of the adults. Claudia and Kimber cooed as if Santa had really appeared. Ray and Ann were waving frantically, and even Noelle was smiling at the man they all recognized.

"I heard," Gil continued in his Santa voice, "that Lea and Lena were having Christmas early this year, and I couldn't let that happen and not drop by. Especially when they have both been such good girls this year."

He sat the girls down and picked up a big red bag he'd brought in. "Let's see what we have for you."

One twin struggled at the tied cords of the bag, trying to help Santa get it open, but the other was standing and watching with a thoughtful expression on her face.

Derrick knew what she was thinking even before she bent and whispered in her sister's ear. The first twin stopped pulling at the cords and stood back to take a good look at Santa.

Satisfied, she shook her head and announced to her sister. "Uh-uh, that's not Grandpa." She began pulling at the cords again, and her sister whispered something else in her ear.

The first twin released the cords and got up on her tiptoes to sniff tentatively at Santa's beard. She frowned. "Is that you, Grandpa?"

Santa's eyes widened in alarm. "No! No, I'm Santa!"

The look on busted Santa's face was so comical, Derrick bit his lip to keep from laughing.

Coming over, Claudia positioned herself between the girls and the bag. "Okay, girls, if you're rude to Santa, he'll take his bag and leave. Is that what you want?"

"No," they whined plaintively. The second twin still stretched her neck to see around her grandmother to Santa.

She whispered loudly to her grandmother, "He smells like Grandpa."

Claudia frowned as Kimber tried to stifle a giggle. "What do you mean?"

The first twin spoke up. "You know, the way he smells when he comes out of his private room."

Ray was smiling, and, seeing his mother's even more

confused expression, he spoke up. "We told the girls that when Dad is in his study, that's his private room, so they can't go in there."

Santa was busying himself with the bag and trying to avoid eye contact with Mrs. Claus. She turned on him with her arms folded over her chest. "You mean Santa smells like Grandpa does after he's been smoking a cigar?"

The girls bobbed their heads, watching Santa carefully, almost certain in what they believed.

Santa decided to come to his own defense. "Ho, Ho, Ho. Like a lot of jolly old men, Santa does like his cigars—let's see what I have for Lena and Lea." Instead of reaching in the bag and bringing out the gifts one at a time, he poured the contents of the bag on the floor. As hoped the two girls dove into the pile giggling gleefully, and any desires to unbeard Santa were soon forgotten.

With a final "Ho-ho-ho" and a wave of his hand, Santa quickly disappeared back through the house. Before the girls had completed their scavenging in the pile of dolls and toys, Gil reappeared, slipping onto the sofa next to his wife. The adults were struggling not to laugh as Claudia discreetly picked a few stray pieces of white cotton lint from Gil's hair.

Sitting there, watching the girls enjoy the day, Derrick found himself daydreaming about one day playing Santa to his own children, with Noelle cast as Mrs. Claus. And Derrick realized that it was the first time he'd had daydreams about the future since Camille visited him in the group home.

That day had been a turning point in his life, and the hope she'd offered had ended up taking his life in a direction he could never have imagined.

Being here with Noelle felt the same. Hopeful.

Chapter 15

Although it was only three in the afternoon, the winter sky made it appear to be late evening as it poured down a mixture of rain, sleet and snow. Derrick stood staring out the living-room window at the wide expanse of flooded lawn that surrounded the front of the large estate home Camille had strong-armed him into buying a few years ago.

He didn't regret the house; it was a symbol of his status in life. Of all he'd achieved since stepping off that bus in front of the Massey Building all those years ago. But on days like this, when the weather matched his mood, the mansion seemed empty and cold.

Especially after having experienced the warmth and love radiating from the walls of the Brown home. Noelle's childhood had been the polar opposite of his, and yet he could not deny the overwhelming feeling of some kind of connection to her. He was certain he understood her. And, reluctant as she might be to admit it, she understood him.

There was lust, no doubt about it. The woman was custom-built for his idea of a good time. He could make love to her every night and never tire of that voluptuous body. Despite that obvious attraction, there was something else; the instinctive trust he'd felt the first time he'd met her.

She felt safe. He felt safe when he was with her.

He could confide his deepest secrets and greatest fears and not be judged. There was no real reason to feel that way; in fact, there was every reason not to.

Derrick knew what little control he had over his own emotions, especially when it came to the women in his life. He was possessive by nature. Being in the group home during his formative years had left a stain that could never be removed. Each boy had little to begin with, and whatever little else you were given, a newer pair of shoes, the occasional toy, you fought and scraped with everything in you to hold on to it. And when your whole personality was formed around the idea of fighting to hold on to whatever you had, it naturally developed a possessive character.

He wasn't exactly sure why this possessive spirit grew to monstrous size whenever the affections of a woman came into the equation, but it did. And now that possessive spirit, coupled with the attraction to a woman he wanted more than he'd ever wanted a woman before, was multiplying exponentially. Trying to imagine the kind of power Noelle could have over him was troubling, but what sent a chill down his spine was the knowledge that one day she might discover it.

His self-preservation instinct said to leave her alone. To accept one of the candidates she put forward and stay the hell away from her. But how could he? When every time he closed his eyes he saw her teetering on the edge of a orgasm in the back of that restaurant, squirming beside him in the back of his car, begging for release, smiling at him in playful invitation as he was temporarily gifted with a pink sweater.

She was everything he'd searched for in a woman. Sophistication and poise, passion and purpose. She was all that and more. And now that he'd found her, he didn't know what the hell to do with her.

With a deep sigh, Derrick turned and headed back upstairs, trying to think of something that would shake his melancholy mood. When he reached the second landing, he headed in the direction of his poolroom.

As he moved from room to room of the large empty house, he thought again of filling it with a family he loved.

Across town, Camille, with the help of Noelle was getting dressed to go on her first date since her husband died.

She shook her head adamantly at the elegant, sequined light pink gown Noelle held before her. "I haven't worn that in over ten years."

"But it's beautiful. Why not?" Noelle smiled, trying to keep her frustration from showing. This was the seventeenth gown that had been rejected. Noelle understood that much of Camille's hesitation was nerves, but nervous or not, Charles would be there in thirty minutes to pick her up for their dinner date.

"It's too…girlish." Camille frowned at it. "No, that will never do."

Noelle returned the pink gown to the walk-in closet and brought out a beautiful white, silk pantsuit.

"Absolutely not," Camille immediately protested. "It's the middle of December, and you expect me to wear white?"

"Camille, no one adheres to those old styles of etiquette anymore."

"Well, I do. I'm not wearing white in the middle of winter."

Noelle turned with hunched shoulders and returned the suit to the closet. This time when she came out of the closet she was empty-handed.

Camille looked slightly suspicious. "Surely, I haven't run out of evening wear already."

"No." Noelle crossed her arms over her chest. "But I've run out of patience. We need to talk." She crossed to where Camille was sitting on a chaise lounge, bracing her elegant mahogany cane between her legs.

"Camille, I know you're nervous. That's perfectly normal. It's been over ten years since your husband died, and you were married for forty years. But you are a vibrant woman, and you deserve someone to spend time with."

Camille busied herself with adjusting her skirts. "I know that. That's why I agreed to go on this little outing. Now we just have to find me something to wear."

"How can we when you are trying to find any excuse not to go through with this?"

"I am not—"

"Camille, what's really going on here?"

"What do you mean?"

Noelle laid her hand over Camille's, where it rested on top of the cane. "Why don't you want to go on this date?"

"Stop calling it a date." Camille frowned down at the hands for several long seconds before shaking her head in defeat. "I don't know. It just doesn't seem right." She glanced at Noelle. "Don't get me wrong. Charles sounds like a charming man, and the thought of having someone to spend time with is very appealing. But…"

Noelle wrapped her arm around Camille's shoulder. "Go on."

"Things were different in my time, Noelle. Women behaved differently than they do today. Royce was…the first man, the only man I ever…knew." She shook her head sadly, and Noelle's heart went out to her, realizing this was much harder than she'd imagined.

She leaned forward to see Camille's face and offered a soft smile. "You mean knew in the biblical sense."

"That's just the way it was done in my time. In a world controlled by men, a woman's virtue was sometimes all she had of value, so she guarded it and kept herself for the man who would be her husband."

"Camille, you don't have to offer me any explanation. I completely respect that." She huffed. "Sometimes I wish I had guarded *my* virtue a little better. No one is asking you to do something you are uncomfortable with. The reason I chose Charles is because in many ways he shares your values and ideas. As I told you before, he is also widowed, after thirty years of marriage to his high-school sweetheart. I'm sure this is not easy for him, either."

Camille's frown deepened. "And that's something else that bothers me. He's a younger man."

Noelle's eyes widened. "Camille, he's sixty-four. You're not exactly robbing the cradle."

A small smile formed on Camille's lips, and before

she could stop it a burst of laughter escaped. "I guess you have a point."

With a small squeeze of her shoulders, Noelle released her and stood. "Whatever happens tonight is completely up to you. You can have a nice dinner, say good-night and never see him again. Or…you can open yourself to the possibility of a new beginning. It's completely your call."

Camille looked up at her with a strange expression. "You're very good at this."

Noelle smiled. "It's my job."

"No." Camille studied her for several moments. "It's more than that. There's a deeper understanding in you. I recognize it because I've seen it before—in Derrick. But you use it differently."

Unable to help herself, Noelle blurted, "What do you mean?"

"Well, you use it to help people, just like now. Just like what you just did with me. Whereas Derrick, he uses it to protect himself. To identify threats and guard against them."

Noelle deflected. "So, should I call Charles and tell him to turn around and return home?"

"No." Camille straightened her posture, pushing her frail shoulders back and holding herself up with the regality of a queen holding court. She gestured to the closet.

"Let me see that camel wool suit again."

Noelle, feeling greatly relieved, headed to the closet. The wool suit had been choice number seven or eight, but even if it took three of four more tries, at least they were moving forward.

Camille's old-school etiquette proved to be the

greatest challenge as she insisted on finding proper shoes and a matching clutch purse to go along with the suit.

Charles arrived at four o'clock exactly and was forced to wait downstairs almost a half hour for Camille to make her way down. But the smile on his face was enough to remove any lingering annoyance Noelle may have been harboring over the laborious duty of getting Camille dressed. The end result was excellent. She looked splendid in the light brown suit and matching low-heeled pumps.

The three left the house together, and as Noelle watched them pull away in Charles's car, she was left with a feeling of intense satisfaction. First dates were always her favorite part of the process. There was so much anticipation, and, as she'd said to Camille, the possibility of a new beginning.

Chapter 16

Derrick sat in the darkened theater wishing he were somewhere else. The lovely young lady at his side kept sending him nervous glances and Derrick found he was growing more annoyed by the moment.

She was another match based on his requirements.

Chandra was sweet and shy, and owned a small boutique downtown, and when she looked at him she had stars in her eyes. She was pretty without being beautiful, with large breasts and nice full hips and a soft-spoken nature, and he wanted nothing more than to bolt out of there.

How in the world had he ever thought a wallflower would suit him?

What was most disturbing was the realization that Noelle was setting him up on dates with candidates that actually would've appealed to him. Before he met her.

Somehow, he thought that after their two dates she would start suggesting women that he would *not* find attractive.

He knew she was hesitant about their attraction, but this was almost as if she were trying to get rid of him. *Was* she trying to get rid of him?

Not that it mattered, he huffed. He had no intention of going anywhere.

The slight sound caused Chandra to look at him with wide, startled eyes. "Did you say something?" she asked quietly.

He forced a smile. "No. Are you enjoying the show?"

She bobbed her head. "Yes, very much, thank you."

He sighed and returned his gaze to the production on the stage. He knew that this whole experience would be different—better—with Noelle. Probably, most notably, because a darkened threater like this would be perfect for a little discreet flirtation. With the right woman of course, he thought, glancing at the woman next to him.

Over an hour later they left the theater and climbed into Derrick's car to take Chandra home. She was silent for the whole ride. He walked her to the door, said good-night, waited for her to go inside and then got back in the car.

Even as Don pulled away from the curb, Derrick was pushing digits on his cell.

After a couple of rings, she answered. "Hello?"

"Sorry, no chemistry. My turn. Dinner tomorrow night?"

Noelle was quiet for several seconds before she blurted out, "Did you even try?"

"Of course."

"Sure, you did. So tell me exactly what was wrong with Chandra?"

"She wasn't you. Dinner tomorrow night?"

"Derrick…"

"Don't try to weasel out of it. We have a deal."

"Fine, but this is the last one."

"We'll see. I'll pick you up at seven."

"Six! I want it over with as soon as possible."

"Don't you enjoy spending time with me?" he teased.

"What do you think?" With that, she hung up.

Derrick couldn't wipe the silly grin from his face. He would take a few minutes of spirited debating with Noelle over a full evening with timid Chandra any day.

As the Lexus pulled up in front of Derrick's elegant home, Noelle looked around in surprise. "Where are we?"

"My home." Derrick enjoyed watching her eyes widen.

"You live here all by yourself?"

"Yes. What do you think?"

"It's beautiful."

Not as beautiful as you. Taking in her calf-length, form-fitting, black cashmere dress. All she wore with the dress was a small string of white pearls and matching earrings, and a pair of black-and-silver strapless stilettos.

Her shoulder-length hair was wrapped in some kind of curly design on top of her head, giving him easy access to the perfect, soft skin on the back of her neck. Tonight she was the essence of understated elegance, and all Derrick could think about was the minimal effort it would take to get her out of that dress. And how much he enjoyed spending time with her.

"But what are we doing here?" she asked as Don came around the car and opened the door. "I thought we were going to dinner?"

"We are." He smiled and gestured to the large double, wood doors at the top of the three wide cement stairs. "Right inside."

Ignoring Don's offered hand, she turned on the seat to look at Derrick. "Why didn't you tell me we were dining in your home?"

"Does it matter?"

He watched as she tried to find a reasonable argument, but she couldn't without stating what she suspected. That he was trying to get her closer to his bed. It was true, of course, but she would never admit that it was what she was thinking, too.

"No, it doesn't." She took Don's hand, and Derrick exited on the opposite side of the car. He dismissed Don for the evening before leading her up the stairs.

As the couple entered the house, Derrick took her overcoat and hung it up in the closet.

Noelle turned in a circle, looking up at the cathedral ceiling with skylights that covered the foyer of the colonial-style mansion. The large entryway was tastefully decorated for the holidays with a tall stately tree in one corner and poinsettias and wreaths on tables and doors.

"Who's your decorator?"

Derrick glanced around as if seeing the foyer for the first time. The simple decorations had a distinctly feminine touch and Derrick knew that was probably what had prompted the question.

"I have a cleaning crew that comes in three times a week. I pretty much give them free rein on that sort of thing. I hadn't even realized they did this."

She frowned. "Did they do it today?"

He shrugged. "No, no one was here today. Probably last week sometime."

"You don't know?"

"I usually get home really late and head straight to bed. I rarely even turn on the light in here." He gestured to the hall leading to the rest of the house. "Shall we?"

As she walked along the corridor, her head turned left and right as she tried to take in everything. His attention was completely trained on her as he tried to take in everything about *her*.

The cashmere dress was perfect for her luscious curves and moved with her body in the most erotic way. As he walked a step behind her, the soft fragrance she wore drifted to his nose. One day he was going to have to ask her to identify that perfume. He thought he was becoming addicted to it.

The high-heeled shoes she seemed to prefer were flattering to her full calves. When he'd first met her he'd assumed she was as tall as he, but he now realized without shoes she was actually a couple of inches shorter. The perfect height to lay her head on his shoulder.

"You have a beautiful home."

"Thank you," he answered absently, watching the soft material of the dress slide over her hips as she walked. She really knew how to accentuate her voluptuous figure.

They came to the large entryway leading to the formal dining room, and she stopped. "Whoa."

Derrick glanced over her shoulder with a sigh. The long table had been completely set for twenty guests. Bright candles flickered from one end to the other.

He'd asked for an intimate setting and gotten a table ready to seat the queen of England. Derrick knew it was his own fault.

He'd made sure the catering service understood that

he was entertaining a very important dinner guest, and apparently they'd taken him to heart.

"Are you expecting others?" she asked.

She stood directly in front of him, and as Derrick moved his attention from the table to her, he realized his lips were only an inch from that beautiful neck. He gave in to temptation. He bent forward and placed a gentle kiss on the spot right beneath her ear. She scuttled forward as if he'd stung her, and covered the place with her hand.

She was nervous. If he had not been sure before, he was now. "Sorry, I couldn't resist."

She frowned at him as if to say *try harder next time.* She held her tongue and returned to her question. "Are we dining alone?"

"Yes." He took in the overdone room once more. "I guess I overstated my needs."

He guided her to the opposite end of the table and pulled out a chair for her. As she took it, he crossed the room to where the two covered heating trays were sitting and removed the covers to reveal two lobsters.

He brought them to the table, sat them before her and watched as her face twisted in horror.

"I take it you don't like lobster?"

She glanced at him pitifully. "I'm sorry, but I'm allergic to shellfish, including—"

"Lobster."

She nodded. "But it looks delicious."

Derrick sat next to her with a sigh. Somehow his perfect evening was taking a drastic turn for the worse. "I should've asked you that."

"It's okay." She laid her hand over his. "It's my loss. It really does look delicious."

Derrick smiled. He was the one who had screwed

up, and yet she looked apologetic. "So, what is your favorite food?"

She smiled shyly and shrugged. "Nothing so elegant as lobster, I'm afraid."

"No?"

"No, give me a good old-fashioned steak sandwich loaded with cheese any day."

"Sounds good to me," Derrick said, pulling his cell phone from his pocket.

"What are you doing?"

"Ordering dinner."

Less than half an hour later, the pair was tearing into large, messy steak subs, and as Noelle took another bite, her eyes closed and she sighed with bliss. Her brown eyes danced with laughter watching Derrick try to maneuver his own sub.

"You know, there really is no respectable way to eat a cheesesteak. You just have to go for it."

"Sorry, habit," he said, taking a bite.

She arched an eyebrow. "That's surprising. You didn't strike me as being too hung up on etiquette."

"When I graduated from Penn State, Camille and Royce took me out to dinner to celebrate. Up until then, we'd only dined together in small diners and fast-food-type places. This time, they took me to Stone and Wilkey and it was the first time my table manners were put to the test." He glanced at her. "I failed miserably. After that, teaching me proper table behavior was added to Camille's growing list of lessons."

"She means a great deal to you, doesn't she?"

"I don't know where I would've ended up without her."

"What made you interested in architecture?"

"It was what Royce did."

"That's it?"

"Yes. If he'd been a baker, I'd probably be tossing dough every day. It's not like I had a ton of role models. I don't regret it. Once I got into it, I learned to love it. So, ultimately, it was the right choice for me. What made you start Love Unlimited?"

"I majored in sociology and became a certified therapist, and for a period I did relationship counseling. Some of the reasons marriages failed were because people married impulsively and then later discovered they were simply incompatible. So I thought, what if there was a way for people to find someone more compatible before they got deeply, emotionally involved?"

"And the idea for Love Unlimited was born."

"Exactly." She wiped her cheese-covered fingers on a linen napkin. "Despite the cash-flow problems, I've been very successful. Eventually, I would like to expand to other states." She glanced down the long table at all the empty seats. "Do you entertain a lot?"

Derrick followed her eyes. "You know, I think this is the first time I've ever used this room."

"Really?"

"I usually just take my meals in the kitchen or the theater room."

Her eyes widened. "You have a theater room?"

Derrick gave her a curious look. He loved that she got excited over cheesesteaks and in-home theaters. "Yes, would you like a tour of the house after dinner?"

She smiled. "Just the theater room. I love movies."

"What's your favorite?"

She glanced away. "Too embarrassing to admit."

She looked so guilty, Derrick was dying to know.

"Really? Hmm. This should be interesting. Let me see if I can guess. Romance?"

"Give up. I won't admit it."

"Action?"

She took another bite and ignored the question.

"Comedy?"

She continued to eat.

"Oh, come on. At least a hint."

Finally, she sighed, her brown eyes soft and seductive, and Derrick wondered if she was even aware how inviting her eyes were.

"Fine. Suffice it to say, I'm truly a hometown girl."

Derrick toyed with that for a moment. *Hometown girl?* He frowned. "*Philadelphia?* That movie with Tom Hanks?"

"Um, no." She returned to her sandwich.

And then it occurred to Derrick, and he burst into laughter. "Don't tell me *Rocky?*"

Her silence was answer enough.

He tossed his arms in the air and began chanting the theme song. "Dunna dun, dunna dun, dunna dun…"

She shook her head in disgust. "I knew I shouldn't have told you."

He leaned forward and placed a quick kiss on her cheek. "You didn't—I guessed."

She only rolled her eyes and Derrick realized he'd gotten away with the kiss. She was becoming more comfortable with him.

"Well, if it's any consolation, my favorite is not any better. Remember that old James Dean movie, *Giant?*"

"I love that movie!"

He frowned in shocked surprise. "Really?"

"Yeah, James Dean is one of my favorites. Too bad

he only made a few movies before he died. He had that something special, you know?"

He nodded, growing more fascinated by the minute. He watched as she finished up her sandwich. He'd been finished with his long ago. She wiped her mouth and hands and smiled at him, and Derrick knew in that moment there was little he wouldn't do to keep that look of contented satisfaction on her face.

"Ready for the tour?"

Yes, she was.

A few minutes later as they were leaving the poolroom, Noelle turned to him. "Derrick, this is really a beautiful home."

"Thank you." He took her hand in his as he led her down the carpeted hallway, and she did not pull it away. When they'd first left the dining room, he'd taken her hand and she'd instantly pulled away. He was learning…gentleness.

This was the real prize. To get her to accept his touch when she was fully self-aware. When she knew he was standing beside her thinking about bedding her, wanting to bed her, and she wanting the same. He would be her lover, with each glide of skin over skin, his fingers skimming along her cheek, his arm around her waist, her hand in his. He could feel her slow and steady capitulation.

He led her into a separate hallway off the main corridor and opened the door. "Watch your step. There are a couple of stairs there," he said, reaching for the light on the wall. When the track lights came on, it revealed a large sunken room, with a huge television taking up one wall.

"Wow." She glanced at the group of leather recliners

positioned in front of the television. The large wood cabinet standing off to the side of the room contained every manner of audio and visual equipment. There was a bar in the back of the room and a large popcorn machine standing in one corner.

Derrick plopped down in a nearby recliner. "You know, when I was a kid, I never even dreamed of having something like this." He surveyed his achievement with pride.

Noelle joined him in the next recliner. "You've overcome a lot."

He shrugged. "No more than a lot of people. But…" He paused, wondering if he should confess what he was about to say. *I'm safe. I'm safe.*

"But what?" She tilted her head, listening attentively.

"I was pretty much illiterate until I was about thirteen. So you see how this is a very unlikely outcome." She continued to listen with rapt attention and before he realized it, he was spilling much more than he'd planned. "When I was first put in the home, Camille came to see me. I was blown away. I never thought I would see her again, and then suddenly there she was. She told me that if I stayed in school and graduated, she would give me a job after high school."

Her brown eyes searched his. "You didn't believe her, did you?"

"Of course not."

"What changed your mind?"

"A birthday card, of all things." He huffed. "After she left that day, I convinced myself she'd only come to ease her conscience. A few weeks later, I received a birthday card, and the message in it said four more to go, stay strong." He glanced at her. "See, there was no reason for her to send that card unless what she was saying was real. It was my first taste of hope, and I loved the way it felt. Having something to look forward to, imagining a real future. On those days when things went…particularly bad, I would pull out that card and reread those words."

"And when you graduated you came looking for Camille."

"And she kept her word."

"I don't know if I would've been able to do that."

Derrick could see the thoughts racing behind her eyes. "What do you mean?"

"It takes a strong person to beat those odds, even with a Camille in your corner. I'm not really that strong."

"Are you kidding me?"

"Seriously. I've always had my family like the wind at my back. Even when I decided to open Love Unlimited, I knew they would be there to support me. I don't know if I could've done it alone. Especially at thirteen or fourteen."

"Noelle, don't underestimate yourself. You're a lot stronger than you think."

"How would you know? You just met me a month ago," she said softly.

Slowly, he reached out and cupped her cheek in his hand.

"Baby, I see it in your eyes. Your metal may not have been tested yet, but trust me when I say it's there. A spine of pure steel." He leaned forward, giving her time to resist and grateful she did not. "I know a survivor when I see one." He pressed his lips to hers and sighed into her mouth as her lips parted beneath his.

Chapter 17

Pulling her against his body, he took her mouth once more. And there was no way she could resist the sweet taste of his mouth.

She wound her arms around his neck, pulling him closer to her, even as her mind shouted that she should be pushing him away.

She forced herself to pull out of the warm shelter of his arms and instantly felt cool air touch her skin. "Derrick, we shouldn't do this."

"Give me one good reason why."

"It will complicate our working relationship."

He gave a disbelieving look. "I said one *good* reason." He reached for her again, but she quickly stepped back.

"I'm serious!"

"Damn—but you can make an easy thing hard!" he exploded in frustration. "What's wrong with two consenting adults making love? We're both single, we're obviously attracted to each other, what's the problem?"

She shook her head in dismay. "The fact that you want me to believe it's that simple."

She watched as he took several deep breaths, trying to control his frustration. "Explain it to me, because obviously, I'm not getting something."

She shook her head. "I knew going out with you was a mistake." She headed toward the door, but his words stopped her.

"What are you so afraid of, Noelle?" He came up behind her. "What has you so terrified you can't even take the chance on us?"

"I know what you are, Derrick."

"Tell me, Noelle, what am I?"

She turned to him. "You're my greatest heartbreak. And frankly, I don't want to go through the pain of getting over you."

"How can you possibly know that's how it's going to turn out?"

"It's all right there." She touched his face, looking into his eyes. "Me! My big body. And your passion, your vengeance, your possessiveness, your unbending personality. It's all written right there."

"I want to make love to you, Noelle, not own you. If tomorrow you decide we have no future, I'll leave you alone. I just want tonight."

"Liar." She turned and began pacing. "Derrick, you don't love women, you consume them. You want to fill every part of them, and when they won't let you, you get frustrated and try to force your way in." She stopped pacing and turned to face him once more. "That's why you have such trouble in your relationships."

He simply stared at the floor.

"Well?" She finally asked. With his eyes downcast, she could not feel his emotions.

"Well what?" He glanced up, and his green eyes blazed with anger. "I'm just listening to all this psycho-babble and wondering if maybe you take your job a little too seriously."

"You're angry."

He returned to the chair he'd vacated earlier. "No, Noelle, just horny." He glanced at her over his shoulder. "It's no big deal. You keep me that way." His hungry eyes roamed over her body. "You're so damn sexy, even when you're not trying to be." He pulled his cell phone from his pocket. "If you want to go, I'll call Don for you. Forgive me for not escorting you home. I don't think I can."

She stood uncertainly in the middle of the room, torn between want and need. She needed to leave. She needed to get out of there before Derrick changed his mind. He'd resigned himself to her leaving. She should go.

The other part of her wanted nothing more than to stay. To comfort him. To make love to him. To be with him for as long as possible.

His eyes came to hers. She wondered just how revealing her own eyes were.

"Are you going?"

The truth escaped her lips before she could stop it. "I don't know."

He smiled. "Poor Noelle, your luscious womanly body just won't cooperate with that Vulcan-like brain of yours, huh?"

She glared at him.

"Tell you what." He relaxed back in his chair, and Noelle could feel the smugness in the air. He thought he was winning. "Why don't we just watch a movie? See how you feel in a couple of hours, and then, if you still want to leave—" he shrugged "—that's that."

She folded her arms over her chest. "And what are you going to be doing for those two hours?"

He licked his pink lips suggestively. "Trying to convince you to stay, of course."

What am I doing? she asked herself for the tenth time, even as she took a seat in the lounger beside him. His handsome face was curved in a faint smile that he struggled to suppress.

"You're trying not to smile, but you feel like you've won."

He huffed. "Trust me, sweet, when I win, you'll feel it, too." He picked up the remote by his chair. "Okay, so, what are we watching tonight?" He clicked the remote and the huge screen came to life.

Soon he had a list of available movies running down the screen, and Noelle was distracted by the number of choices.

They settled on an action movie she'd never seen before but Derrick assured her she would enjoy. It turned out to be a foreign film with lots of martial-arts action, and halfway through, with a small bowl of buttered popcorn on her lap, she was enjoying it and Derrick's company.

It was always surprising to her to realize that Derrick, who normally seemed so surly on the surface, was in fact quite the comedian when he let his guard down. He had a quick wit and keen observation skills, and nothing seemed to escape his notice.

Not even her internal struggle to resist his charm.

He sighed. "Beauty, why do you fight it so?"

She shifted her body back in the direction of the screen. "I told you why."

"Okay, how about a different scenario?" He placed his own bowl of popcorn on a nearby table. "What if I told you that all the things you said about me in that case file were true, but in your case, none of those factors would be an issue?"

"Do you really think I'm that gullible?"

"What if I told you that none of those factors would be an issue because I'm a different man when I'm with you?"

"Sure you are."

He leaned forward. "Sometimes I feel like I have this raging storm inside me that I can't control. It's been that way all my life. With you, there is a kind of peacefulness. There's something about you, Noelle…. You calm the storm."

Derrick Brandt had a habit of saying the wrong thing at the wrong time, but when he managed to get it right, he *really* got it right. Noelle did a mental shake to break free of the hypnotic trance he seem to be able to cast over her.

He shrugged. "So maybe I am all those things you said earlier, but you don't have to worry about me breaking your heart, because with you those things would not apply."

"What happened to just for tonight?" she taunted.

"You know what happened. You saw right through that. No, you read me right the first time." He glanced at her, his green eyes clearly visible in the dim light. "I'm playing for keeps."

They watched the movie in silence for a few moments before he spoke again. "So, tell me about this paragon you're looking for."

"What paragon?"

"Mr. Perfect. The man you'll give your heart and your body. The man we mere mortals could never compare to."

"Ha-ha."

"I'm serious."

One look in his eyes, and she knew he was.

"Tell me about him."

"What can I tell you about a man I haven't met yet?"

"I assume you know what you're looking for."

"I *do not* want to have this conversation with you."

"Why not? If I'm going to be dismissed so quickly, I at least deserve to know my competition."

"Just watch the movie."

"Why don't you want to talk about him?"

She stood, and, once again anticipating her move, Derrick stood with her.

"This is silly. If you're going to spend the rest of the night badgering me out of spite, I might as well go home now."

"It's not spite, Noelle. I just want to understand why the woman I think just might be the one for me *knows* I'm not the one for her."

"You're so stubborn." She threw up her hands in surrender.

His arm snaked around her body before she realized it and he was pulling her against his body. "Yes, I am. Especially when there is something I really want. And I *really, really* want you, Noelle—and not just for one night." His hot mouth came down on hers and Noelle kissed him back.

As she placed her hands on his shoulders, she began to realize how natural he was starting to feel. The taste of him, the feel of his body against hers. She was becoming accustomed to the way they fit together.

Derrick's other arm came around her body, cupping her bottom and pressing her against his erection. "Give us a chance," he whispered in her ear, right before his hot tongue traced a line from her ear to her collarbone.

She struggled to control her breathing as she felt his large hand working its way beneath the soft material of her dress.

"Stay the night with me, Noelle." He planted little kisses along her cleavage line, and her head fell back in surrender, just as it did every time he did that. She responded to his touch as if hardwired to him. "Please, sweet, for both our sakes, stay with me."

She acquiesed with just a slight nod of her head, but it was enough. Derrick stopped his sensual assault and took her face between his hands to look directly at her.

"Yes?" he asked for clarification.

Her body still strumming from his remembered hands, she quickly nodded again, and he pulled her against him, reclaiming her mouth with renewed fire.

"Yes." Noelle cast all doubts aside, pressing her body against his and reveling in the feel of his throbbing organ pressed against her.

Derrick stopped, pulled away and took her hand, leading her to the door. "My bedroom is just down the hall." Together they walked hand in hand down the hall.

He pushed open a set of double doors and Noelle found herself standing in the middle of a large master-bedroom suite. Her eyes quickly scanned the mahogany wood furniture and emerald carpet before falling on the large bed that dominated the room.

Derrick came up behind her, his busy hands working the cashmere dress up her thighs. "I've been thinking about this since the moment I picked you up," he whispered in her ear, but she barely heard him as her mind was following the hand that worked its way around her body and slid into her panties.

Suddenly his fingers were pushing her lips apart, working their way to the center of her being. Unable to keep her balance, Noelle reached around and grabbed hold of him for stability.

"You won't regret this, Noelle." He continued to seduce her with words as his other hand worked its way up her body to cup a hardened nipple between his fingers. "I promise you won't regret this."

She closed her eyes as he worked his hand into her dress, beneath her bra, to press flesh against flesh.

She felt him surrounding her on all sides, playing her body like a cello, even as his fingers slipped inside her wet center and stroked her to the point of no return. Noelle widened her stance, wanting him to have access to all he desired. Wanting him to never stop stroking her, even as she felt the explosion building in her core. With her head resting on his shoulder, Noelle was in a daze of sensual pleasure. "Der…Der…"

"Shh." He manipulated her soft sexual flesh between his fingers. "Don't speak. Just feel."

That was fine by her, because it was all she could do. She rolled her head against his shoulder, not knowing how to express the absolute pleasure of feeling his fingers inside her. His erection throbbed against her backside, and her nipple hardened to a pebble in his hand. It seemed like the feeling was so intense, so extreme, that she could barely breathe—and then she stopped breathing.

As the universe exploded around her, her body bucked and pushed against Derrick's hand, desperately seeking a completion that he was more than ready to give.

Holding her solidly against his long body, he stroked her tender flesh until she was crying for mercy, and only then did he cover her mouth with his. She slowly descended back down to earth and took a breath.

Chapter 18

Lost in a haze of satisfaction, Noelle barely noticed Derrick pulling the dress up over her head and sliding her panties to the floor. He led her to the edge of his bed and gently pushed her to a sitting position. Kneeling before her, he carefully took off each shoe and massaged her feet.

He stood silently before her for so long that Noelle curiously looked up at him and was surprised by the fierce expression on his face. He was thinking about something intensely.

Finally, he reached out and ran his hand along her face. "No one has ever responded to me the way you do." Then he was crawling across the bed, covering her body with his, his attentive mouth returning to hers.

She slipped her arms around his slender waist, pulling the shirt from his pants. He was chiseled, all muscle and energy.

She ran her hands beneath his shirt and he sat up on his haunches and quickly pulled the shirt over his head, revealing a chest rippling with muscles. In silent fascination, Noelle ran her hands over the contours, sliding her fingers through the curls that covered his upper body, narrowing to a path leading down into his trousers.

"You're gorgeous," she said, in awe of his masculine beauty.

He just smiled, most of his attention focused on releasing her bra. It didn't take him long to open the clasp and pull it down her arms, his eyes roaming over her exposed skin.

"There's even more of you than I thought." He quickly replaced his hands with his mouth, sucking, teasing and pulling on her breasts.

As she wrapped her arms around his back, accepting his heavy weight, Noelle knew she was surrendering more than just her body. She was accepting Derrick and all his volatility into her life, into her heart, into her soul.

He knew it, too. He sat up on his elbows, looking down at her. He said nothing, just stared at her for several moments, but she understood.

There would be no fooling each other or themselves into believing this was a fling. This was commitment, real and possibly lasting, and whatever else happened tonight, it would mark the beginning of something that would endure beyond morning.

His mouth came down and touched hers lightly, drawing her into the kiss, forcing her to acknowledge with her body what she could not with her mouth. She was every bit as entangled as he was.

"I can't wait, baby." Suddenly his comforting weight disappeared. He stood beside the bed removing his slacks and briefs, and then he was searching his nightstand. He quickly found a condom and began slipping it on.

Her eyes took in his exceptional rod. Somehow she'd known he would be made like that. His manhood was as impressive as everything else about him.

Something occurred to her. Her eyes narrowed. "I see you keep those handy."

His mouth twisted, even as he concentrated on the task. "Don't even go there. I have an almost full box. Wanna see?"

"Almost full?"

"Oh, come on. I only met you a month ago." Fully erect and covered, he put his knee on the bed. "Cut me some slack."

Seeing his beautiful body looming over her, knowing soon all that throbbing heat would be inside her, it didn't matter who'd come before. Only this moment mattered.

She opened her arms, welcoming him into her body, into her life, into her heart, and with a soft smile he accepted the invitation and lowered over her, guiding himself into her.

On first penetration, Derrick paused, his head buried against her neck and Noelle thought she would die of anticipation if he did not complete what he'd started. Holding him around his smooth back, she shifted her body to allow him to sink deeper.

He growled against her neck. "Don't move. It feels good, baby, doesn't it?"

Noelle could feel his pounding heart against hers, but she wanted him all the way. He kissed her neck. He lifted his body enough to bring each of her legs around his waist, then sank into her until the curly hair covering his groin met hers. Slowly, carefully, he pulled his hips back, sliding out of her body until only the tip of his penis was connected to her, and then pushed into her fully, exploding.

Noelle could feel his orgasm even as it triggered her own, and her body arched against his, coming up off the bed to meet him. Derrick wrapped her in a tight embrace and held her close as his body trembled and trembled, and finally, empty and exhausted, his heavy weight collapsed on top of her.

An hour later, Noelle opened her eyes. It took her a moment to realize where she was. She felt something across her waist and reached down to find Derrick's arm across her body.

The room was still light, since neither of them had bothered to turn off the switch before falling asleep. She turned her head and watched his sleeping form. The man really was as handsome as sin, everything from those too-soft lips to his ridiculously lush eyelashes.

She thought about the earlier part of the evening, dinner and the movie, and how much she'd thoroughly enjoyed his company. And then her mind wandered to the last and best part of the night. She closed her eyes, remembering every detail of his brief but powerful lovemaking. It was even better than she'd thought it would be, and she'd thought it would be really good.

No, she had never questioned their physical connection. It was the terrifying emotional attachment that frightened her. She'd never felt this way about a man.

Derrick stirred beside her, and she turned to him again to find those intense green eyes trained on her face.

He watched her for several seconds, before a smile finally spread across his face. "Hi."

She smiled back. "Hi."

He bent forward and kissed her. It was a playful, light kiss, but it immediately caught fire, and he deepened it.

Suddenly, he sat back and looked at her again, but this time there was a thoughtful expression on his face. "What's wrong?"

She frowned. "What do you mean?"

"You're worried about something."

"What makes you think I'm worried about something?" she asked warily. It was this kind of thing that scared her about this man. He was much too attuned to her.

"I can feel it. So, what's wrong?"

"Nothing. What do you mean you can feel it?"

He shrugged. "I just can, and you're lying."

She said nothing, because she knew exactly what he meant. She could feel his emotions. Noelle silently wondered how two people so wrong for each other could've formed this kind of a connection.

"You're not…regretting it, are you?"

She could see his vulnerability in his eyes, and she quickly shook her head. "No, of course not."

"Then what?"

"Derrick, what's your favorite color?"

"What?"

"Favorite color."

"Blue."

"What shade?"

"What are you talking about?"

"Blue is my favorite color, but I like powder. You?"

He sighed. "Royal, I guess."

"What do you value most?"

"Noelle, what's going on?"

She pulled the blanket closer around her body and

shrugged dismissively. "Just trying to learn something about you." She gestured to their situation. "Given the circumstances, I thought it was appropriate."

"What are you talking about? We know plenty about each other. What's all this about?"

"It's just...I feel a little like I went to bed with a stranger."

He scooted closer to her. "Noelle, you know more about me that almost anyone in this world. I've told you things I've never told anyone. And maybe there are things about my history I haven't told you, but that's because there are things I don't know. Am I prone to certain medical conditions? Who knows? But the important stuff you know."

She lay staring at the blank ceiling, but she could feel his eyes on her.

Suddenly he said, "Whatever you're dealing with, Noelle, come to grips with it, because I'm not giving you up."

She turned on her side to face him. "That's not what I meant."

"What then?"

"I don't know." She closed her eyes, hoping she could end the uncomfortable conversation.

She felt his weight shift off the bed, and when she opened her eyes the lights had been turned off.

Then he was crawling into bed behind her. His warm body encircling her, his arms wrapping around her, she felt his lips on her shoulder and shuddered with a growing need he seemed to be able to always produce in her.

She heard the wrapper being torn in the dark, and her heart sped up as she anticipated what was to come. Then hands were everywhere. On her breasts, curving over her waist to find her moisture. A soft sigh of pleasure escaped her lips and Derrick took it as some sort of sign.

He shifted her position and slowly, carefully, penetrated her from behind. Noelle knew she would never get enough of the feeling of him. She was developing a severe addiction to this man with a history of bad relationships, but she couldn't stop herself. He felt too good, too right, and with each gentle push into her body, he proved to her that she was not as strong as she had once thought.

Soon he was sliding in and out of her with ease, and the pleasure pulsating in her middle once again seemed unbearable. But she held on, chasing him to the edge of the abyss.

Derrick's arm tightened around her waist as the rocking motion of their bodies took on a life of its own, and then he was arching against her back and pouring himself into her.

Lying over her shoulder, he kissed her neck once and whispered "You think too much" in her ear, right before falling to sleep, still buried inside her body and holding her against him.

Chapter 19

Over the course of the next week, Noelle immersed herself in her work, trying to block out all the chaos rattling around in her brain.

She closed her eyes, remembering the feeling of him buried deep inside her body. Even now, sitting alone in her office, she craved him. This was just what she'd feared. Derrick Brandt was becoming a habit.

It was another Saturday afternoon, and she was once again trying to catch up on all the paperwork. It was three days before Christmas, and this was always a busy time of year.

The phone began to ring and she glanced at the caller ID and saw that it was Derrick's cell phone. She started to pick it up, but paused. She was still not quite ready to deal with him. She needed more time to think. It rang three more times, and then the voice in her office doorway startled her up out of her seat.

"So you *are* ignoring me." Derrick closed the cell phone and returned it to his pocket. "You know, I thought that might be the case, but then I thought…hey, she's an industrious entrepreneur, maybe she's just really busy."

"What are you doing here?" Her hand went to her midsection, feeling the throbbing of him even as he stood several feet away with that hard glare in his glowing eyes.

"I'm here to find out why you're ignoring me."

"I'm not ignoring you."

He tilted his head to the side, watching her. "You say that even after what I just witnessed?"

She crossed her arms over her chest as he began to move across the room toward her. "What do you think you witnessed?"

"You not taking my call."

"I'm busy. I have a business to run."

He stopped and just stood there for several moments staring at her, and it was one of those rare times when she could not decipher what he was thinking.

He turned and returned to the door. She was certain he was leaving until he closed the door and locked it. Turning back to her, there was a new determination on his face.

"Somehow we've ended up back at square one." He started toward her again. "I think you need a refresher course."

The way he moved told his intention. "What? You gonna sex me into submission?"

He grinned in that devious way of his. "It's a dirty job, but somebody's got to do it."

She felt her heart skip a beat, but tried desperately to control it. "Derrick, I don't have time for this nonsense. I have work to do."

"You should know that the fact that you're calling our lovemaking nonsense only encourages me to continue."

"Derrick, I'm serious."

He rounded the desk. "So am I."

She tried to back up, but his long arm snaked around her. "Now, what's going on? I thought we'd conquered this particular mountain, and here you are rebuilding it."

She settled in his arms, grudgingly satisfied to be there. "There's nothing going on. I've just got a business to run."

"So do I. But it's not more important than you."

She glanced at his eyes. There it was again. That terrifying honesty and raw emotion that acted like a catalyst for her own.

He nibbled at her neck, and the soft touch sent a shiver down her spine and made her want to damn-near purr. "Talk to me," he said quietly.

"I have nothing to say."

"Sure?"

"Yes," she whispered, and swallowed hard, trying to control her rapidly beating heart and ignore her throbbing center.

"Good." He lifted her by the waist and sat her on the desktop. "I didn't really want to talk anyway."

In record time, he had her skirt up and her thighs parted. A practical part of her brain realized if she really wanted to stop Derrick from taking control of her life and her will, she really would have to invest in some pantsuits—they were harder to get into.

"Derrick," she moaned even as he began his tender assault on her face and neck. "We can't do this here." Hearing her own voice, Noelle knew she didn't mean what she was saying, and Derrick knew. She glanced down at the sound of the wrapper tearing, and then his hands were there on her center, pushing her panties to the side as he eased into her body.

Without protest, her hips lifted to him, allowing him to sink deeper. Using his arm, he pushed her files out of the way as he laid her back on the desk.

Still fully clothed except for the intersection of their bodies, Noelle looked up into his revealing eyes, watching the emotions play out before her. He kissed her again, holding her mouth captive, simulating the actions of his body with his tongue. Noelle clung to him, and holding her hips tightly he plowed her wet center with fierce intent.

"Oh, Derrick, yes, yes!" Noelle felt the tremors course through her body like a little internal earthquake, and then Derrick followed with his own climax as he poured himself into her.

Later, condom disposed of and their clothes readjusted, Derrick sat in her chair. His large hands rested on her hips where she sat on the edge of the desk.

"I was originally calling to see what your holiday plans were. Camille's having a small dinner Christmas Eve, and she invited us."

"Oh." She glanced at her electronic calendar, which happened to be up on the computer monitor. "Just a casual dinner with my folks, but I'm sure I could cancel. I'll see them on Christmas Day, anyway."

He gently stroked her thigh. "You need to work out whatever doubts you may be having, Noelle, because this thing between you and me is good. Why you have such a problem with it, I don't really understand."

"I don't understand, either," she confessed. "I really like you, Derrick, and I really like being with you."

"But?"

"But as a relationship counselor, I've watched a lot of

couples who looked good fall apart anyway. People who have intense chemistry and nothing in common never make it. That's why I started Love Unlimited, to help people find their common-interests mate. And it works."

"We have things in common."

"Hot sex and a love of movies?"

"It's a start."

"But is it enough?"

"You really do think too much."

"Maybe. It's just…I'm starting to really care about you, and I don't want to be hurt."

"Do you realize you are setting us up for failure? Instead of just enjoying the moment, you keep anticipating our downfall. We can't control tomorrow, Noelle, only what we do with today."

"I know that."

"So, what? Am I supposed to just leave you alone?"

She glanced at him to see what he thought about that idea.

He huffed. "Rhetorical question. Ain't gonna happen."

"I need to get back to work." She tried to move away, but he wouldn't release her.

"Know what I think?"

She paused, waiting.

"I think you're more afraid of *feeling* than you are of *thinking*. I think that you hide your emotions behind a wall of logic and reason, and it terrifies you to experience real, raw emotion." He stood. "You can't reason love, Noelle. It defies logic, and it has no specific rhythm or reason, despite your success with Love Unlimited. Love is not just common interests and a dash of chemistry. It's intense. It's overwhelming." He leaned forward so that he was at eye level with her. "And…it's unstoppable."

Chapter 20

The Lexus pulled to a halt in front of Camille's elegant suburban estate home.

Noelle turned her head and found Derrick watching her as he'd done off and on since arriving on her doorstep thirty minutes ago to pick her up for Christmas Eve dinner at Camille's home. It was the first time she'd seen him in the two days since their encounter in her office. She had not received so much as a phone call.

Not knowing how else to deal with those watchful eyes, she smiled.

He didn't return the smile. "You look beautiful tonight."

"Thank you." She reached over to touch his open shirt collar. "You're looking quite the snazzy picture yourself."

Just then Don came around and opened the back door, and Noelle, accepting his hand, stepped out of the car. A few moments later, Derrick had joined her on the steps leading to the front door.

"Has she lived here long?"

His arm slithered around her waist. "As long as I've known her." He paused, looking up at the huge home. "I can still remember the first time she and Royce brought me here. I'd never seen anything like this. I thought for sure I'd stumbled upon some kind of African royalty."

"The way Camille was ordering me around her bedroom the other week, I can see why. Will Charles be here? I heard they were getting along."

He frowned.

"You have a problem with Charles?"

"No, no problem," he muttered.

"Good." Her eyes narrowed on his face. "For Camille's sake, you should probably keep it that way."

Just then the front door opened, and there stood a gray-haired man in his mid-sixties. He was several inches shorter than either Noelle or Derrick, but his stocky frame was well-toned and reflected years of athletic interest.

"Charles." Noelle smiled. Slipping away from Derrick, she came forward to greet her client. "It's so nice to see you again."

The older man returned the smile and gave her a hug. "Good to see you, especially under these circumstances."

Derrick came up beside her. "Charles."

Charles's smile faded briefly. "Hello, Derrick."

Noelle looked back and forth between the two men, trying to understand the obvious tension between them. Then Camille appeared beside Charles.

"Charles, why haven't you invited them in?" She gestured with her arms.

Noelle entered the house and hugged Camille. "Thank you for having me."

"Thank you for coming." She kissed her cheek, then whispered in her ear, "And for Charles."

Derrick was closing the door behind him when Camille turned to hug him. "Merry Christmas, Derrick."

Derrick returned the hug, squeezing her tightly. "In light of our additional guests, are we continuing our tradition this year?"

"Tradition is tradition." She smiled up at him and Noelle realized this was the second time she'd ever seen them together. The love between them was obvious.

"What tradition?" she asked.

Charles spoke up. "Apparently Camille and Derrick have a tradition of decorating the Christmas tree on Christmas Eve."

"Actually, it was a tradition started by Royce, Camille's late husband." Derrick offered, and Camille's frown told Noelle she was not the only one who noticed his inappropriate tone.

Charles nodded without missing a beat. "Yes, she did mention that."

"Why are we standing here?" Camille interrupted. "Into the living room, everyone." She shooed them forward.

Derrick and Noelle went ahead of the slow-moving older couple. Taking advantage of their moments alone in the room, Noelle turned to him. "What is your problem with Charles?"

Derrick answered eagerly. "She is a seventy-year-old wealthy widow." His green eyes glittered with anger. "What do you *think* my problem is?"

Just then, Charles and Camille came through the door and it was obvious Charles was adjusting his pace for Camille's slower movements. With Camille's guidance, they added decorations to a large evergreen tree. Derrick explained more about Royce's tradition. In fact, it seemed to Noelle that he was going out of his way to mention Royce Massey as often as possible.

As he reached over her head to hang an ornament in the top of the tree, Noelle whispered, "Cut it out."

"What?" he said, instinctively snuggling against her neck.

"The Royce thing you're doing to aggravate Charles—stop it."

Instead of answering, he placed a quick kiss on her neck and moved away to collect another ornament.

An hour later, as they were eating dinner, he started again with what the holidays were like when Royce was alive. Camille and Charles simply chose to ignore him, but Noelle could not.

Right before her eyes he was reverting to the jackass she'd met that first day in her office.

Outside of Derrick's bad behavior, dinner was a pleasant experience. Noelle enjoyed watching Camille and Charles interact and took a bit of pride in knowing that she was the one who'd brought them together.

Shortly after seven, Noelle and Derrick were saying good-night and heading home. As they started out the door, Camille grabbed the back of Derrick's coat, and Noelle heard her say quietly, "Tomorrow you and I need to have a long talk, young man."

Derrick exchanged a terse good evening with Charles and guided Noelle down the stairs to his car.

Once they were driving away from Camille's home, Noelle turned to him. "Okay, what's your problem with Charles?"

He arched an eyebrow. "What do you know about that guy?"

"As much as I know about you. He's a client, and a very nice gentleman."

"What does he do for living? How does he make his money? I assume he has children. How long has he been widowed?"

"Whoa." She put up a defensive hand. "What do you think? I matched Camille with some kind of geriatric gigolo?"

"Of course not."

"Then what's wrong?"

"She's been on her own for over ten years now, Noelle. And before that she was married to the same man for *forty years.* Camille is a highly intelligent woman, but if Charles was some kind of money-grubber, she wouldn't even know what to look for."

She put up two fingers. "One, you underestimate Camille. And two, you underestimate me!"

"What are you talking about?"

"I take great pride in my ability to match couples, Derrick! I put a lot of effort into seeking out compatible traits—and by *suggesting* that I would somehow match Camille to some kind of male black widow—"

Suddenly he was reaching across the seat and pulling her against his side. "Shh, I'm sorry. Settle down. I'm sorry."

Noelle wanted to protest, but it felt too good being back in his arms.

"It never occurred to me you would take this personally, although I should've known. It's just that I worry about her." He kissed the top of her head. "I'm sorry, I didn't mean to question your professionalism. Forgive me."

Noelle snuggled against his chest, accepting his apology. How could she ever do anything else?

Chapter 21

As they arrived back at the brownstone, Noelle waited on the curb as Don handed Derrick a large box from the back of the car.

"Thanks, I'll call you in the morning." Derrick dismissed the driver for the night, but Noelle knew he would be there bright and early to pick him up.

"What's that?" she asked, as he carried the big box to the door.

"You'll see." He had a mischievous grin on his face as he waited for her to open the door. Derrick carried the box into the living room and placed it on the floor next to the couch. "Got any candles?"

"In the kitchen." She studied the box for a moment. "What are you up to?"

He grinned. "Go get the candles, and I'll show you." She went into the kitchen and dug around in her junk drawer until she found a few votive candles and carried them back to the living room. She saw a smaller cake box sitting on the middle of the coffee table. The big box was still sitting on the floor, and the flaps were closed.

He frowned at what she was carrying. "I meant birthday candles."

"This is all I have." She came forward. "A cake?"

He opened the box. "Your birthday cake."

She kneeled beside him on the carpeted floor and was surprised to see her name scrawled in powder-blue writing across the white icing. "It's not my birthday."

"I know. Your birthday is February nineteenth." He took the votive candles, sat one in the middle of the cake and, drawing a lighter from his pocket lit it. "For all the birthdays I could not share with you. Happy birthday."

She simply stared at the glowing candle, and then at Derrick, who sat crossed-legged by the table, waiting. "Aren't you going to blow out the candle?"

"This is so sweet." She threw her arms around his neck, squeezing him close. "Thank you."

Derrick kissed her neck and pushed her back. "Blow out the candle, before we burn the place down."

Noelle leaned forward and quickly blew out the candle.

Once she did, Derrick reached into the big box once more and pulled out another small box, wrapped in birthday paper, with a large powder-blue bow on top, and handed it to her.

"What's this?"

"Open it and see."

Noelle opened the box and was amazed to find a brand-new Raggedy Ann doll inside.

She tilted her head in confusion.

"I understand you had one as a little girl, up until your dog—Demon, I think his name was—destroyed it when you were sixteen, right? According to your mom, you were distraught about it because you'd planned to keep the doll for your own daughter."

Noelle felt her heart skip a beat. "Derrick, what's all this about?"

He took her hand in his. "You say I don't know you and you don't know me. Tonight, we start working to change all that. I'll try to tell you anything you want to know."

The sincerity in his eyes was like a soothing balm. He was trying to cross the bridge to her. It was more than she'd expected.

Not ready to respond to that statement, she changed the subject. "You spoke to my mom?"

He coughed loudly. "And your dad. Interesting man."

"He can be." She laughed, imagining what her parents must've thought when Derrick called looking for information about her.

He began counting off his fingers. "Your favorite color is blue—powder-blue. Your middle name is Marie, like your mother's. You had four pets as a child—the forenamed Demon dog, a parakeet named Tweety, a cat named Munchkin and another dog, named…" He popped his finger, trying to remember.

"Demon Two." She smiled.

"Right. How could I forget that?"

"You know, you don't have to do this."

"I think I do. That man you read about in the papers, that's not me, Noelle." He shrugged. "That's not completely true. Yes, it was me. But it was a me I never wanted to be." With a deep sigh, he sat back against the couch. "I'm possessive, and there is not a whole lot I can do about it. Growing up…so few things were mine. If you didn't become protective and possessive, you never got to keep anything. There was always a bigger, tougher boy ready to take what was yours."

"But women aren't things, Derrick."

"No, sweet, they're much more precious—at least to me." He arched an eyebrow. "And if I wasn't willing to share my toys with other boys, how the hell do you think I feel about the idea of sharing my woman's body with another man?"

Noelle toyed with the doll's red hair, wrapping her mind around what he was saying.

"Noelle, try to understand. Those women you read about… Honestly, I'm not sure I loved any of them. It was about keeping what's mine. I would hear or see some man trying to move in on me, and those deep instincts would take over. What I felt for them was so different from what I feel for you. You can't judge me based on what you've read."

"That's not it." She shook her head.

"Then what?"

"Sometimes I feel like the more I'm with you, the more I become like you and less like me. And that scares me, because I don't know enough about you."

"What do you mean?"

"I feel like…" Her mind raced as she struggled to find the right words. "I feel like you're leading me somewhere, but I don't know where. I care about you and want to go, but I'm afraid at the same time."

He leaned forward. Pulling her fingers loose from the doll's hair, he wrapped her hand between his. "You would rather stay where you are. Where it's safe."

She glanced up into his expressive eyes and knew he understood. "Sometimes."

"Sweet, love is not safe. It's not always about staying in your same little comfort zone."

"Are you sure this is love and not just lust?"

"I've had lust. Lust is nothing but a quick hit. But with you…I'm satisfied just breathing the same air."

Noelle could feel herself melting. She straightened her spine as if that could bolster her weak will. "But let's be realistic, Derrick. As a matchmaker—"

"Stop right there." He held up his hand. "You're about to go wrong already. We're not two strangers you are trying to put together, Noelle. Matchmaking is good when you're trying to *find* the right person. But we've found our right person. Now we just have to find a way to make it work."

She glanced at the cake sitting on the table. "We can't learn everything about each other in one night, you know?"

"I know. I was wondering if you did. You once called me the X factor, remember? I've been satisfied with you since the first time I noticed your so-called wedding ring was missing." He frowned. "Why were you wearing that thing anyway?"

Her mouth twisted in a smirk. "To avoid guys like you."

He laughed. "Oh well. So much for that, huh?"

She couldn't help but smile in return. "Yeah, so much for that."

Later that night, spooned against his body in her bed. Noelle's heart was filled to the brim with love and hope, and for the first time since becoming intimate with Derrick, she was content. "Derrick? You awake?"

"Yeah." His warm breath brushed her ear.

"I just wanted to say thank you for earlier, for trying. It meant a lot to me."

"You mean a lot to me."

She smiled, remembering the rest of the contents of the box. The four huge bags of trail mix, which he'd learned was her favorite snack food. The copies of the James Dean movies and the entire *Rocky* series. The three large volumes of *Endangered Wildlife* illustrations that he discovered were her passionate cause. She was amazed to realize he'd compiled all of it in only a couple of days.

"Derrick? What made you want to go out with me? I mean, what first attracted you to me?" She rolled her eyes, feeling his large hand cup her bare breast.

"Enough said," he muttered against her neck.

"I'm serious."

"So am I. I had a really hard time keeping my hands off of you at the first meeting. You kept leaning across the desk, putting them in my face. It was driving me crazy."

"Damn, I'm going to have to watch that. No, I mean, when did you know?"

He was silent for so long, she wondered if he'd fallen asleep. "Derrick?"

"Are you trying to start a fight?"

"What?" She turned over on her back to try to see his face in the dark. "Why would you think that?"

"Here we are doing good, enjoying a nice cuddling, and you start with the *when did you know* questions."

"I was just wondering."

"No, you were trying to *reason it out,* as usual. Why can't you accept that sometimes love is just... counterintuitive."

"I don't know." She frowned. "You said your possessiveness was just something I was going to have to get used to. Maybe my need to make sense of things is just something you're going to have to get used to."

"Fair enough."

"Did you mean all that stuff you said in our first meeting?"

"All what stuff?"

"Self-supporting, and wide hips, all that nonsense."

"What nonsense? You're a successful entrepreneur, and—" his hand slid down over her hip bone "—and this is one fine pelvis. You'll have no trouble at all making babies."

"But then you were talking about a wife."

Suddenly he leaned up on one elbow. "I still am."

In the shadows of the moonlight coming in the window, she could see his fierce expression. "Things have changed since then. You were looking for a match."

"And I found one. A woman who is exactly what I want in a wife."

She forced a smile. "It's too soon for that kind of commitment."

"Why?"

"We've only known each other a month."

He studied her face for several long minutes. "Fine. We can move slow, just as long as we're moving."

Chapter 22

"That was interesting," Noelle laughed as Derrick led her out of the Kimmel Center for the Performing Arts. "The whole body-art thing was um…unexpected."

He huffed. "Unexpected is not the word I would choose." He stepped down from the curb to signal to Don they were ready before turning back to Noelle. "Weird, strange-as-hell, a waste of my money, are all better descriptions than *unexpected*."

"Hey, don't be so hard on them, they really tried." Noelle was feeling pretty forgiving of anything as she stood shivering with cold on the city sidewalk outside the theater.

The past few days with Derrick had been better than anything she would've imagined.

Derrick, seeing her shivering with cold, returned to where she stood on the sidewalk and put his arm around her shoulders. Just then a camera flash went off in her face, temporarily blinding her.

She blinked rapidly, trying to get her bearings, and suddenly felt Derrick move away from her.

"Get the hell out of here!" he was growling at someone, and there was a slight commotion around her as someone else touched her arm. She opened her eyes and realized Don was standing next to her.

"This way." He quickly motioned her to the car, and Noelle hesitated.

"But, Derrick—"

"He'll be along in a moment. He asked that I get you in the car."

By then, Noelle's vision had cleared and she could clearly see Derrick half a block away in pursuit of a man who was running at top speed to stay ahead of his pursuer. Suddenly Derrick stopped running and stood watching his prey escape.

All around her, finely dressed theater patrons crowded the street. Many were chattering in groups, some were pointing in Derrick's direction and others were staring at her.

"What's going on?" she asked Don in confusion.

"Just a photographer." He gestured to the car once again. "Probably freelance." Noelle took his lead this time and climbed into the car. "Don't worry. Mr. Brandt's an expert at dealing with the press," Don said right before slamming the door shut.

Noelle was not so sure. As the warmth of the heated seats settled into her chilled bones, it suddenly hit her. The photographer had succeeded in getting a picture of her snuggled up with Derrick.

She closed her eyes in dismay, thinking of the possible

headline in tomorrow's tabloid. This was what she'd feared most. That her association with Derrick would become fodder for trash magazines. The kind that seemed to love Derrick Brandt and his spontaneous outbursts, such as chasing photographers down busy avenues.

The door opened and Derrick sat down hard next to her. "Get us out of here, Don," he said before reaching over to pull Noelle close. She resisted.

He turned to look at her and let out a heavy sigh. "Here it comes. Say it."

"Say what?" She pulled her wool coat closer around her, refusing to take his bait.

"Whatever it is that has you so angry. I didn't *know* he was going to take that picture, and I tried to get the film back, but he's a little faster than the last one." He studied her expression. "What?"

"Nothing," she muttered.

"That's not what your face is saying."

Unable to hold back any longer, she turned to face him on the leather seat.

"Why did you chase him, Derrick?"

"I just told you, to get the film back."

"But don't you see? Chasing him only drew more attention to you than if you'd just let him go. All the people we'd just watched the show with were staring at the spectacle of you chasing the guy."

"Is that your problem? That I made a spectacle of myself?"

"Yes! It is!" Noelle was seething with a frustration she could not explain. "That type of behavior is what has made you such a social pariah."

His eyes widened. "Social pariah?" He turned to look out the window. "Damn. That's harsh."

Noelle instantly regretted her words, but had no way to take them back.

The rest of the ride to her brownstone was quiet. As they pulled up in front of the building, Derrick glanced at her but said nothing.

He opened the door and stood. By the time Don came around the car, he was helping Noelle out. "I'll call you in the morning," he said.

Noelle felt a sharp disappointment until she realized he was talking to Don. Derrick took her arm to lead her to the stairs of her brownstone and she pulled back slightly.

Derrick instantly felt her rebellion and whispered in her ear. "If you want to keep me from making a *spectacle* of myself, you'll wait until we are inside to express any dissatisfaction you may have with me."

She said good-night to Don and bit her bottom lip to keep from telling Derrick good-night. As much as she would hate to admit it, he was right. The last thing she wanted was to give her neighbors a show. As she turned the key in the lock, she heard the Lexus pulling away. She went inside, tossed her purse on a nearby hall chair and turned to face Derrick just as he was turning the dead bolt.

Before she could get a word out, Derrick crossed the room and took her in his arms. His soft lips came down on hers, and with shameful little resistance she returned the kiss. Regardless of whatever else went on between them, this touching, this connection, would always feel right.

He stepped back and smiled. "I thought I better get mine before you let loose."

That small comment and the smug satisfaction on his face was enough to remind her of her anger.

"Derrick…" She took a deep breath, determined to

speak reasonably and rationally and not let her emotions lead her. "Derrick, you have to understand that when you do things like chase reporters through crowded streets, it…looks bad."

He frowned. "So, what was I supposed to do? Smile for the camera."

"Don't be ridiculous. Of course not! But try to conduct yourself with something resembling dignity."

He shook his head and headed to the kitchen. "Here we go with this dignity thing again. I'm not you, Noelle."

"I don't expect you to be me." She followed. "But you are one of the wealthiest men in Philadelphia."

"What does that have to do with anything?" He reached into the fridge and grabbed the juice bottle. Before he could turn it up to his lips, she snatched it away.

Crossing to the cabinet, she took down a glass. "The fact that you have to ask that question says exactly what it has to do with it." She poured the juice into the glass and handed it to him. "Derrick, you're a thirty-five-year-old successful businessman. Your days as a juvenile delinquent are over!" She reached up and gently tapped her index finger against his temple. "But not in here!"

"So now I'm a social pariah *and* a juvenile delinquent." He took a sip of juice. "Don't stop now, baby, you're on a roll."

Noelle stared at his handsome face, trying to understand how an evening that was going so wonderfully had become so bad, so fast. "I guess being with you…something like this was inevitable."

"I guess so." He drank the last of the juice and turned to place the glass in the sink. "So, what now?" He turned back to her.

Noelle was immediately taken aback by the hard glare in his eyes.

"The couch?" he muttered.

"What do you mean?"

"You're angry with me, so am I to assume I'm banned from your bed? That is how you women try to control us, isn't it? Cut off the sex?"

Noelle was mentally trapped somewhere between exhaustion and rage. "Do you really think I would do that?"

"Wouldn't be the first time it's happened." He shrugged. "But understand this—I won't force my way into your bed, but I won't leave, either. Even if I have to sleep on the couch."

She sighed in exhaustion. "Derrick, you don't have to sleep on the couch. But the truth is, I'm not feeling very amorous right now. So you're welcome to stay, but sleeping is all we'll be doing."

"You serious?" His hard eyes bored into hers. "You won't make me leave?"

"Of course you can stay—if that's what you want," she said, looking into his revealing eyes. He was expecting to be rejected, was, in fact, poised for it.

"It's what I want," he said with a nod. "Just don't push me away."

Noelle couldn't help wondering what dumb-ass woman had tried to control him with sex. She stepped closer and took his face between her hands. "No matter how crazy you make me, I will never, ever try to use sex as a weapon. Okay?"

He wrapped his arms around her waist and pulled her tight against his body. "When that photographer snapped that shot tonight, the first thing I thought was how unhappy you would be if that picture showed up in a

tabloid, so I reacted on instinct. I tried to get the picture
back." He buried his face in her curls. "It was a stupid
thing to do, but I didn't know what else to do. I'm so afraid
any little transgression could take you away from me."

Noelle wrapped her arms around his neck and held
him even tighter. Sometimes the man's vulnerability
seemed like a thing that was almost tangible, and the
honesty of his feelings was raw and somewhat unnerv-
ing, especially compared to her, someone raised in a
world of subtlety and nuance.

She guessed Derrick hadn't had anyone to teach him
subtlety and how to control his impulsive instincts,
something most children learned in grade school. What
little he knew of self-discipline and control came from
his own efforts. He was a self-made man in every sense
of the word, whereas she'd spent most of her life cradled
in the bosom of a loving family.

They were so different, in so many ways, many of
which seemed insurmountable. If she'd *matched* them as
a couple, she wouldn't give them even odds of surviving.

"Come on, let's go to bed." Taking his hand, she led
the way down the hall to her bedroom.

Derrick had set his watch alarm to go off at six in the
morning. In his underwear and dress slacks, he crept to
the front porch and found the paper.

He picked it up, and quickly pulled out the Arts and
Entertainment section. There it was: a grainy picture of
them, his face twisted in an angry scowl, while Noelle
looked like a deer caught in headlights. The caption
read: *Bad-boy builder Derrick Brandt and female companion out on the town.*

Derrick quickly shredded the paper in large sections

and dumped it in the kitchen trash before carrying the trash bag out to her Dumpster. Once that was done, he dressed and wrote a note explaining that he would be right back.

An early-morning walk along a quiet city street was the perfect place to think, and Derrick took advantage of the time.

For the first time in his life, he'd been at peace. Waking up beside her warm body filled him with such satisfaction. He didn't fully understand it himself. All he knew was that he wanted to keep feeling this way. He wanted to keep making love to her. He wanted to keep being as they were. And all of that was now being threatened by wheels he'd inadvertently put into motion long before they met.

By the time he headed back to the brownstone, Derrick knew what he had to do. Somehow he had to speed up the hands of time and convince a woman who'd only known him a month that she was meant to be his bride. He had to get her down the aisle before she got her fill of the media and all the other aspects of his life. He had to seal the deal.

The problem was, he wasn't dealing with just any woman. Noelle was a professional matchmaker. And despite the incredible lovemaking, he knew convincing her to marry him would not be easy.

Somehow, he had to find a way, because he'd waited too long for a woman that made him feel the way she did. He'd been looking for her all his life. And he knew she had been looking for him, too.

Chapter 23

"You can't drive?" Noelle was wide-eyed in amazement. "Are you kidding me?"

Derrick, standing on the front steps of his elegant suburban mansion, watched in frustration and embarrassment. "Do I look like I'm kidding?"

"How is that even possible?" she asked. The stunning discovery had come as a result of their decision to take a ride in the countryside. Noelle had suggested they leave the gas-guzzling Lexus and Don the driver and take her lightweight Mariner. As she started to toss Derrick the keys, he announced that she would have to drive because he did not have a license.

"What's the big deal? You can drive, so it's no problem," he said, deciding to turn the tables.

"I just don't understand—"

"You don't need to. Just get in the car." Without

another word, he opened the door and climbed into the passenger seat.

As Noelle took the driver seat, she shook her head. "So, Don drives you all the time, everywhere. Talk about job security."

"Noelle." He sighed in frustration. "Am I going to have to hear this all afternoon?"

She laughed openly. "Probably. Not many men in your position that can't drive a car. Why didn't you ever learn to drive?"

He turned in his seat to face her. "You're not going to let this go, are you?"

"Afraid not."

"Fine." He took a deep breath. "When I aged out of the group home, I had only one thing on my mind— finding Camille. Right away, she helped me get enrolled in school, and between working at the firm and school, I barely had time to sleep and eat."

He glanced at her hoping that answer would suffice. Her curious expression told him it would not. "Then, when I graduated, Royce brought me up from the mailroom as a co-op, and all I cared about was learning everything I could about the firm. I wanted to prove to Royce that they had not made a mistake in helping me. Ten years or so passed, and…Royce died, and Camille offered me a limited partnership, and soon I had no need to drive myself anywhere."

"Wow." She shook her head in awe. "That's crazy. A thirty-five-year-old man who can't drive a car."

"You make it sound like I'm some kind of circus freak," he snapped. "Just let it go!"

Realizing he was really growing angry, Noelle tried to rein in her curiosity. And her laughter. "Sorry." She started the engine. "I didn't mean to upset you." She started down the long drive to the entrance gate.

Halfway down the drive, she stopped the car and put it in Park. "Out," she said, before releasing her seat belt and opening the door.

"What are you doing?"

"I'm going to teach you how to drive."

"Noelle, enough of this nonsense. Get back in the car. It's getting late. If we want to go anywhere today, we better get going."

"Look, we can drive out to Amish country anytime. Today, you learn how to drive." She climbed out of the small SUV, walked around the front of the vehicle and opened his door. "Out."

Derrick's green eyes fairly overflowed with annoyance. "Why is this such a big deal to you?"

Noelle thought about it for a moment, and finally said, "Honestly, I don't know. Except that over the past month you've given me so much, and this is something I can give you."

"Fine." He stood. "One lesson and you let this go. Agreed?"

"Well, let's see how the first lesson goes."

"Noelle...I mean it."

She kept her silence. What was to be gained by participating in a debate she had no intention of conceding?

Almost an hour later, they were tooling around the upscale neighborhood, at the impressive speed of fifteen miles an hour.

"You're doing great. You're a natural!" Noelle smiled, but Derrick did not see it. His complete attention was concentrated on the empty road before him, his large hands positioned at ten and two on the steering wheel.

"This is…. not terrible." He glanced over at her and winked. "Thanks for making me do it."

"Long as you understand that this is only a preview of things to come."

Carefully, he put on the turn signal and turned onto the road leading back to his mansion. "What's that supposed to mean?" He braked at the corner stop sign and looked in every direction before beginning the turn.

"That in the future, when I insist you do something— don't fight me."

Derrick laughed and pulled into his driveway. "Yes, ma'am."

Derrick rounded the redbrick horseshoe drive and pulled to a stop at the front door.

Although she'd been there several times, the beauty of the colonial-style home and beautifully tended lawns that stretched in every direction once again struck Noelle. "How did you find this place?" she asked, looking up at the large white columns that lined the front entryway.

"I didn't. Camille did." He put the car in Park and turned off the ignition. "She walked into my office three years ago and announced I needed a house." He released the seat belt but made no attempt to get out. "Then she proceeded to tell me what I needed in a house. Something elegant and refined in a way that I am not."

"She didn't actually say that?"

He arched an eyebrow. "Wanna bet?" he huffed. "She also said I needed a place to entertain important clients, and…" He glanced at her midsection before reaching over to run his large hand over her flat stomach. "And one day, I would have a family, and I needed an appropriate place to bring a new bride."

Noelle quickly released her seat belt and, opening her door, slipped out of the car and out from under that possessive hand. Derrick, following her lead, got out and came around the car.

"She's really been a big part of your life, hasn't she?" Noelle asked as they climbed the wide concrete steps to the front door.

"Why don't you want to talk about our future?" Derrick asked, walking beside her.

As they approached the front door, Noelle was forced to stop and wait for him to unlock it. Instead, he leaned his long body against the door and crossed his arms over his chest. "Well?"

Noelle didn't know what to say. How to describe the deep-seated fear that occurred in her heart every time she considered a future with Derrick...or worse, a future without him.

"Derrick, we've only been going out a few weeks now. There is no future to speak of at this point. How could we possibly know if this could be anything long term at such an early stage?"

Derrick twisted his mouth in a thoughtful expression. "A matchmaker once told me that a relationship is forty percent chemistry, and if the chemistry is right, it's instantaneous."

Noelle gave him a knowing look. "She also told you that the other sixty percent is compatibility."

"Are you saying we are not compatible?"

"I'm saying I'm hungry. Now open the door so we can heat up those leftover lamb chops you were bragging about."

Derrick studied her face for a long time before pulling the ring of keys from his pants pocket. As he unlocked the door, he called over his shoulder, "You won't be able to avoid this conversation forever. Eventually, you're going to have to make a choice about us."

The word *choice* brought back the conversation she'd had with Kimber the day they were packing up her apartment. She'd said something along the same lines. *You have to make a choice.*

A few minutes later, as the chops were heating in the oven, and they worked side by side on a mobile island preparing a small salad to go along with them, Noelle's mind was still racing with doubt and questions.

Derrick was so wonderful in many ways. He'd overcome great disadvantages to build a life that was impressive by any standard. Unfortunately, like all people, much of his nature had been formed in those early years of life. And there were aspects of his personality Noelle knew he would never completely overcome, such as his impulsive nature and quick temper. Despite the beautifully tailored suits, expensive cars and elegant home, there was an aspect of him that was raw and primitive and would always be that way.

Once there was a time when Noelle would've instantly been able to call to mind a list of qualities that would outline her most compatible mate. Even though that list was no longer as precise and clear-cut as it once was, she was still fairly certain Derrick held precious few of those qualities. That was what the rational, reasonable part of her had to say on the subject.

The woman in her, that part that ruled her heart and soul every time he touched her or looked at her a certain way, that part of her didn't care about any stupid list. Only the sense of satisfaction that came from being with him. Like they were now, just being together doing something so inconsequential as making lunch. Being curled up on the couch as they watched a movie, lying beside him at night, rolling over to wrap herself around his warm body. There was no way to classify or quantify those things, except to define it as that imperceptible something known as chemistry. Was it enough to hold them together for a lifetime?

A half hour later, they were curled up on the leather couch in his large theater room watching the new Will Smith movie after devouring their hastily prepared lunch.

Thankfully, Derrick had chosen to abandon the topic of their future for the time being, and Noelle allowed herself to simply revel in the enjoyment of being with him. Curled against his chest, with the sweet smell of his cologne flowing over her senses, she knew that whatever the future held for them, at this moment she was happy. She didn't know if it was the kind of happiness that could last, but that didn't seem to matter at this point.

Regardless of what tomorrow would bring, she could no longer deny the obvious. Regardless of how irrational it might be, or how doomed to failure their relationship might be, the unspeakable had occurred. She had fallen completely, and hopelessly, in love.

Chapter 24

Noelle squeezed her sister tight, even as she was also being crushed by her other family members who surrounded them on all sides. She was certain that, to the travelers passing by them in the busy airport, they looked like some kind of multilimbed creature.

The day had finally arrived. Kimber was leaving for Los Angeles, and although Noelle had still not completely resolved her own feelings about the matter, the distress the departure was causing her parents forced her to put aside her own concerns for their sake.

Her mother was a mess. According to their father, she had not stopped crying since early that morning. Noelle thought that made sense, seeing how stalwart and strong she'd been up until now, completely unlike their emotional mother.

Of the Browns now gathered together—which included everyone except the twins, who'd already been dropped off at day care—Noelle and her father, Gil, were the only dry-eyed ones in the bunch. Even Ray's eyes were suspiciously glassy.

Kimber was not making the transition any easier, providing her own waterworks, but thanks to the efficiency of the airline, they were soon forced to rein in their emotional farewell as they watched her board the plane on last call.

Fifteen minutes later, the boarding bridge was removed and the airplane was taxiing down the runway. They watched as long as possible before separating and heading in their different directions.

"You are coming to dinner Sunday, right?" Claudia grabbed Noelle's arm before she walked away.

Noelle kissed her mother on the cheek, knowing that, like a mother hen, she would need to see her other chicks quite often over the next few weeks to feel secure. "Yes, Mom, I'll be there."

Seeing Ray and Ann attempt to slip away, Claudia dropped Noelle's arm and headed after them.

"Ray!" Claudia called down the corridor, and Noelle smiled to see her brother's head droop and feet stop.

She turned to her father, still standing with her, and kissed his cheek. "'Bye, Daddy. I need to get to the office. I'll see you Sunday."

"How are you doing?" His thick brows crinkled in a concern that Noelle did not understand.

"Fine. Why?"

He rubbed his grizzled beard. "I saw a picture of you and Derrick in the paper, and you didn't look happy in it."

Noelle fought her frown, knowing it would only concern her father more. She forced a smile. "Oh, that.

That's nothing." She made a dismissive hand gesture, although she felt anything but dismissive.

Now that the word was out that Derrick Brandt was seeing someone, the press was showing up in the most unexpected places at the most unpredictable times, and the number of cameras seemed to be increasing at an alarming rate. The first time, there had been one camera; last night there had been four or more. It was hard to tell when the flashes were going off in quick succession right in her face.

Even worse, Derrick's behavior toward the intrusions had not improved at all. He was still fighting the cameramen, struggling to get their film away and generally making the matter worse.

"How's he treating you?" Gil asked, still watching her face for signs of trouble.

She held the smile in place. "Fine, Daddy, he treats me very fine. Now, really, I have to get going." She kissed him again, thankful to know that the same knight who slayed the dragons under her bed was still on the job. "I love you." With that she headed toward the outside doors and the parking lot that adjoined the airport.

On the way back to the car, she phoned the office and picked up her messages from Terri. She was considering the day's business as she fished in the bottom of her carryall bag, looking for her keys.

It was because she had her head down, looking in the bag and not watching where she was going, that she did not see the two men who jumped out of a nearby van as she approached her car.

One of the men blocked her path. "Noelle Brown? Are you Noelle Brown?"

Without thought, she answered. "Yes. Do I know you?"

"The owner of the Love Unlimited call-girl service, that Noelle Brown?" He poked a microphone in her face.

"Call-girl service?" Only then did she notice the video camera the other man was holding braced on his shoulder and trained on her face. "I don't run a *call-girl service!*"

"We were told that you provide call girls for high-profile businessmen and politicians—is that true?"

She attempted to block her face from the camera and push her way past the men. "No! It's not true!" She pushed hard to get to her car, but the reporter blocked her at every turn. "Move! Get out of my way!"

"And that you yourself are the lover of Derrick Brandt, the well-known architect?" He continued to pound her with ludicrous questions.

Noelle finally reached her car and, not saying another word, forced the door open and climbed in, even as the camera, pressed against the window, continued to film. She quickly put her SUV in Reverse and sped out of the parking lot.

Derrick raced down the hospital corridor until he came to the nursing station. His heart was pounding and he was frantic with worry. He approached the first nurse he saw.

"My name is Derrick Brandt. I was told—"

"One moment, sir." The nurse put up a finger and turned to another nurse who was standing beside her. The two were deep in some kind of argument.

Derrick looked in every direction for someone who could help him now. He approached another nurse coming out of a room. "My name is Derrick Brandt. I was called a few minutes ago. I was told my—"

The first nurse came up behind him and touched his

shoulder. "Mr. Brandt, I'm the one who called you. I'm Nurse Zawlewski."

Derrick turned on her with wild eyes. *"Will someone tell me what the hell has happened?"* he exploded.

His roar seemed to silence all the commotion of the busy station, and for a brief moment there was nothing but a deafening silence on the floor.

Nurse Zawlewski took his arm. "Come with me. I'll tell you everything I can, and then I'll find the doctor for you. How's that?" She spoke in her most comforting tone, and Derrick was surprised to feel the calming effect of it.

Once they were in a small break room, she shut the door behind them. "Mr. Brandt, you were listed as the emergency contact for Camille Massey."

"Yes, yes—is she all right?"

"We believe she's had a heart attack."

"A heart attack?" His legs were no longer able to hold him, and he slumped down in the closest chair. "Is she…alive?"

Nurse Zawlewski touched his shoulder. "Yes, right now she's stable. I'm going to go find the doctor, and he'll be able to tell you more." She headed out the door, and paused. "Will you be all right until I get back?"

He nodded, before burying his face in his hands. The indomitable Camille Massey…a heart attack? He'd almost lost her. She was alive, that's what the nurse said, and that was what he had to cling to. She was alive. But for how long?

Noelle peeked out the front-window curtains of her brownstone once again, hoping against hope that the mob gathered there would give up and go home. They had not.

The phone pressed to her ear gave the same dial tone and message it had repeated the last twenty times she'd tried to call Derrick. Straight to voice mail.

Why is his phone off? It's never off.

She was on the verge of tears, and Derrick was nowhere to be found. The reporter who ambushed her at the airport had aired the film he'd taken on the noon broadcast, and as a result every other reporter in the city was now camped on her doorstep, thinking they had stumbled on the biggest story to hit their town in years.

A high-end call-girl service that provided women to wealthy men.

Somehow, in the short amount of time, they'd managed to get her client list, which contained some of the most influential people in Philadelphia, and that only reinforced the notion that she was running some seedy, backdoor brothel.

Finally, she gave up calling Derrick and tried her attorney. Within a few moments he was on the line; apparently he'd been watching the news and was expecting the call. He suggested she continue to stay hidden for the rest of the day, they would meet in the morning, and he would hold a press conference later that day. She also called the office and told Terri to lock up and go home.

Before nightfall, both Ray and her father had called in concern, but she pleaded with both of them to stay home and told them of the attorney's recommendation that they not give the press anything more to work with by arriving at her front door. Reluctantly, they agreed. Both expressed their displeasure with what they perceived as Derrick's abandonment. Noelle tried to argue, but since she *was* feeling abandoned, she knew they did not believe her.

Shortly after six the media began to disperse, hearing rumors of the attorney's plans to hold a press conference.

As she curled up in her empty bed that night, still having no idea of where Derrick was or why he was not responding to her calls, Noelle gave in to a rare fit of emotion and self-pity and cried herself to sleep.

For one brief moment in her life, it had seemed like all the stars were aligning in her favor. She had a struggling but growing business, contentment in her life and a loving family surrounding her...and then Derrick Brandt had appeared. Demanding, taking and ultimately destroying everything that had come before him.

She'd allowed herself to believe in the impossible, the greatest folly, and now she would pay for it, alone in her bed with her world crumbling around her.

Chapter 25

It was shortly before dawn, and Derrick stood watching the sunrise when he heard stirring from the bed. Quickly he crossed the room to the bed, just as Camille opened her eyes.

Frowning, she asked, "Derrick? Is that you?"

He sat on the side of the bed, taking her hand in his but careful not to rub against the intravenous needle embedded in her arm. "Yes. How are you feeling this morning?"

"As well as can be expected, I guess." She glanced around. "What hospital am I in?"

"Thomas Jefferson." He reached over and pressed the nursing-station button to alert them that she was awake. "Do you remember what happened yesterday?"

"A little." She tried to lick her dry lips, and Derrick went to get the water pitcher the nurse had left over an hour ago on her rollaway table. "I was at home and feeling some chest pain."

Derrick glanced at the door, wondering if he should wait for the doctor to explain the rest, then decided to go ahead. Camille was not a patient woman. "You had a heart attack."

"A heart attack?" She instinctively touched the area between her breasts, and felt the cords running under the gown that covered her chest. "I don't remember having a heart attack."

He handed her a cup of water, placing it carefully between her hands. "Well, you did."

"How did I get here?"

"Maureen called 9-1-1 and me." Derrick said a silent prayer for whatever wisdom had made him stand up to Camille and insist she have a live-in nurse when she'd fought him on the issue.

"Poor thing, she's probably a nervous wreck. Is she here?"

"No, she came by last night, but I told her to go on home and to cancel your appointments."

"Good. She's calmer when she's busy." She took another sip of water, looking at him over the rim. "Why are you here and not running my business?"

"The business can wait."

"Spoken like a majority stock holder," she teased, and Derrick thought it was as good a sign as any that she would make a full recovery.

A slight knock on the door, and the nurse came in. "Good morning, Mrs. Massey. How are you feeling today?"

"Fine," Camille muttered, and Derrick smiled at the annoyed expression on her face as the young nurse hurriedly took her vital signs.

"The doctor will be in to see you in just a moment," the nurse said on her way out of the room.

"Robert's on his way," Derrick offered as comfort once the nurse was gone.

Camille nodded her approval before falling back on the pillows.

After what seemed like an eternity, the door opened and an older man in a white coat came in. "Derrick?"

Derrick lifted his head and was relieved to see a familiar face. "Robert." He stood to shake the other man's hand. "I'm glad they called you."

Dr. Robert Simpson had been Camille's doctor for years. "Sorry I wasn't there to greet you when you arrived. I was in consultation with the cardiologist. Derrick, Camille, you've had a heart attack, or more specifically a coronary spasm."

"What does that mean?" Camille asked.

"The coronary artery constricts or spasms reducing the blood to the heart. It also caused some damage to the right atrium of the heart."

"Please, Robert, cut to the chase. What does it mean? Is she going to be okay?"

Camille listened intently.

Robert nodded. "With the insertion of a device called Automatic Internal Cardiac Defibrillator she should be able to resme her normal, healthy lifestyle."

Derrick exhaled. "What the hell is that?" He was hanging on to his patience by a thread.

Robert placed his index finger and thumb together to show the size of the object. "It's a little round device that goes under the skin in the upper chest wall, and it has electrodes going to the heart. It's programmed to make the heart beat regularly—so if the heart slows down or doesn't beat like it's supposed to, it will give it a little jolt to help it along."

Derrick frowned. "Sounds like a pacemaker."

Robert nodded. "Yes, an artificial one. With it, she should be able to live a long, active life."

Camille smiled faintly. "That's good news." She grasped Derrick's hand. He held it to his chest. Now that Camille was out of the woods, all he wanted to do was call Noelle and and share everything with her. No cell phones were allowed, so he'd have to call her later, maybe when Camille fell back asleep.

That small bit of activity seemed to have wiped her out. Soon she was snoring softly, and Derrick realized right away it was a deeper sleep than she'd been in all night.

He turned his attention briefly to the local news on TV. A few seconds later, he bolted out of the room in horrified shock as the breaking news story of a secret high-end brothel run by the mistress of Derrick Brandt was broadcast in all its seedy detail.

Derrick paced frantically outside the front of the hospital, listening to the incessant ringing of Noelle's home phone, then her cell phone, then her office phone. He tried continually for over forty minutes before giving up.

He was torn between hopping in his car and racing across town and staying with Camille. Finally, he closed the cell phone and returned it to his pocket.

The horrible things he'd just heard on the television upstairs continued to run over and over in a continuous loop in his brain. He couldn't imagine what Noelle must be feeling this morning. He needed to be with her.

He headed toward his car, and stopped. What if

Camille went into surgery this morning and something went wrong? He would never forgive himself if he left her when she needed him most.

How did it come to this? Derrick thought. *Being forced to choose between the two women I love?*

He headed back into the hospital, and, as the elevator doors opened, Charles was standing inside the crowded elevator, having apparently come up through the underground parking lot.

"Derrick." With one glance, Charles took in Derrick's rumpled appearance, his unshaven jaw, his tired and red eyes. "How is she?"

Derrick ran a hand over the new growth that covered his face. "They have her scheduled for surgery at ten," he said, stepping into the elevator.

"How risky is this surgery? And don't BS me!"

The other passengers in the elevator turned at the harsh tone of voice.

Derrick could see the worry and stress on the man's face, and for the first time realized that Camille's affections were apparently being returned. Derrick touched the older man's arm. "Wait until we are upstairs, and I'll talk to you in detail."

He could tell Charles was about to insist, then held his tongue. A few moments later, they reached the floor and stepped off together. As soon as the elevator doors closed, Charles turned to him. "Talk to me, Derrick. I need to know—what is involved here?"

He filled him in on Dr. Simpson's news. "They claim it's pretty routine. They say they don't anticipate any problems. But it is major surgery, Charles."

Charles's lips thinned. "Thank you." He glanced at

Derrick. "I know you don't particularly care for my relationship with Camille, but thank you for talking to me."

Not knowing what to say, Derrick directed him down the hall to Camille's room. The two men moved swiftly, their minds racing with their own concerns. By the time they reached Camille's room, Derrick had decided what to do.

Before he had a chance to open his mouth and say anything, he took in the shocked expression on Camille's face. Her pretty face looked as if it had aged ten years in the few minutes since he'd left her.

He followed her eyes to where they were glued to the television positioned against the wall. He started into the room, and her eyes shot to his face.

"What are you still doing here?" Her shrill voice was filled with unshed tears. "Do you see *what lies* they're telling about Noelle and her agency? Get out of here!" She made a frantic hand gesture. "Go! Go find her!" It had been his instinct all along.

Feeling more relieved than he could imagine, Derrick took one last look at Charles, knowing he was leaving the first woman he'd loved in the hands of someone who would care for her. Then he turned and charged back down the hall.

Over an hour later, Derrick bounded up the stairs to Noelle's brownstone. He banged loudly on the door, calling her name. He banged for five more minutes before abandoning the brownstone and heading across town to her office. He finally ended his search at the Brown family home.

As he came up the walk toward the large wood-frame house, her father and Ray stepped out on the porch, closing the door behind them. The hard stares and defensive stances of both men told Derrick the whole story.

He stopped at the bottom of the steps, looking up at both men. "Is Noelle here?"

He knew the answer even before Gil Brown gave him a solemn nod.

"Will you tell her I'm here?"

"Where were you last night or even this morning?" Gil asked, his deep voice gruff with anger.

"My business partner—my…my…my mother— had a heart attack," he announced. "Will you tell Noelle I'm here?"

Ray looked at his father, and Gil gave him another one of those decisive nods. Ray turned and went back into the house, leaving Gil and Derrick alone.

"I'm sorry to hear about your partner," Gil said quietly. "But my little girl needed you last night when all this stuff jumped off."

"I know." Derrick fought to keep his temper in check. After the last twenty-four hours, his emotions were as raw as an open wound. He knew that Gil was only speaking as a concerned father.

The door opened and Noelle stepped outside, and Derrick finally released a breath he hadn't realized he'd been holding.

Her father whispered something in her ear and then went back into the house.

Derrick did not move from his place at the bottom of the stairs, still unsure as to his welcome. Inside, he was dying to take her in his arms.

As Noelle finally made eye contact, Derrick watched as the hostility in her brown eyes turned immediately to concern.

"What's wrong?" she asked.

"Camille had a heart attack yesterday."

Instantly, she was bounding down the stairs, straight into his arms, and Derrick welcomed her as a damned man embracing salvation. He closed his thick arms around her, holding her as close to his heart as physically possible.

Wanting to pour all his anguish into her welcoming arms. "Noelle, I'm so sorry—I didn't know about the story until this morning. Cell phones aren't allowed on the hospital floor, so I just turned it off. Can you ever forgive me for not being here for you?"

Instead of answering his question, she countered with her own. "How is she?"

Derrick knew it was a bad sign, but instinct told him not to push her. "Stable. They are doing surgery this morning to put in a pacemaker."

"You should be with her!" She stepped out of his arms and frowned at him.

He smiled for the first time in two days. "She said the same thing about you."

Stepping even farther away from him, she wrapped her arms around her body. "I'm fine. You should go be with Camille."

"What the hell happened?" he asked quietly. "I turned on the news this morning, and all I saw was something about Love Unlimited being a escort service, and—"

"Apparently, a rumor was started that I was some kind of madam running a high-end call-girl service, and then they got access to my client database and it all kind of unraveled from there."

She stated the entire crisis so matter-of-factly she could've been reciting what she had for dinner the night before, Derrick thought. He reached out and tilted her chin so he could see her eyes, and what he saw there froze his blood.

Nothing.

No anger, no pain, no sadness…just a blank expression.

"Noelle…what can I do? Tell me, baby, what can I do to help." He moved to put his arms around her, and she quickly stepped back out of reach.

"Nothing at this point. But thank you for the offer. My attorney suggested I get some of my most loyal clients together, and we will do a press conference explaining, and hopefully it will do some damage control. Unfortunately, several clients have already tried to disassociate themselves from me."

"Why are you talking to me like I'm just anyone? I'm sorry I wasn't here last night, but I'm here now. Tell me how I can help you."

For the first time since she'd stepped outside the house, her eyes flashed with emotion. Intense anger. "I just did."

"Not as a loyal client! As your lover. As your friend. Or better yet, just tell me who first reported this?"

She licked her lips, and he noticed the slight shaking that seem to be running through her whole body. "Derrick, I really don't need to deal with your drama right now. Just go."

Derrick balled his fist at his side, trying to keep from taking her in his arms. She was in pain. Now that he could see through the cracks in her armor, it was so obvious. "Baby, please don't close me out. I need you right now."

She finally exploded in rage. "I can't worry about *your needs* right now. I have too many of my own!" She turned away from him, closing in on her own body.

He watched as her shoulders began to tremble. She

gave in to the tears she'd apparently been fighting to hold back. Derrick was so stunned by the outburst he didn't know what to say. Once again, he tried to put his arms around her, and once again she rejected his touch.

Finally, she turned to him with a tear-streaked face and said, "Go to Camille, Derrick." She turned and rushed back up the stairs, calling over her shoulder, "She needs you more than I do."

Chapter 26

Four days, twelve phone messages and ten e-mails later, Derrick was still no closer to getting Noelle to talk to him. He was forced to watch with the rest of the world as she took on the media with her attorney by her side, only doing what he could behind the scenes.

Using his own connections, he'd found out which reporter and which news station was first to "break the story," and using strong-arm tactics he hadn't used in years, he was working his way backward and was certain he was close to finding the origins of the lie.

And once he found that person...

"Derrick?"

Derrick turned at the sound of his name to see Camille being rolled along the hospital corridor by an orderly. She was looking beautiful in her shale-blue pantsuit. Her hair, wrapped in a scarf instead of one of her wigs, was the only sign that she was still feeling slightly under the weather. She did not look like a seventy-year-old woman who'd just undergone major surgery.

Despite his tremulous emotions, Derrick forced a smile. "Enjoying the royal treatment?" he teased.

"Not at all," she humphed. "I'm more than ready to return home." She glanced past him to the sliding glass doors. "Is Don here?" She sounded slightly concerned.

Derrick was unable to hide the smirk on his lips. Camille knew of the driving lessons he'd been taking, and he knew her confidence in his newfound ability was shaky at best.

"Right out front." He took her small leather tote bag from the orderly.

They went through the sliding doors to the curb where Don was waiting with the back door open on the Lexus. He smiled as Camille was rolled closer.

"Good to see you, ma'am," Don said in greeting.

"Not nearly as good as it is to see you," she muttered, already struggling to get out of the chair.

The orderly quickly locked the wheelchair in place, and Derrick offered her his arm. "Camille, slow down. I know you feel good, but you should take your time."

"Oh, Derrick, I hope you are not going to turn into a overprotective pain in the butt."

Derrick ignored the slight chuckle of the orderly as he guided Camille into the back of the car. "Call me names if you want, but I still say slow down."

A few minutes later they were headed home, where Maureen would be waiting. Derrick had also taken it upon himself to hire a few more household staff. Camille might think she was well able to resume her usual routine, but he was not about to take the chance that she was not.

It didn't take her long to start in on him.

"Have you talked to Noelle?"

Derrick glanced at her, wondering if she was trying to annoy him, but it was genuine concern on her face. "No. She won't take my calls or return my messages."

"Have you gone to her house?"

"Yes. She won't let me in."

"The agency?"

"Camille, I've tried to talk to her, she doesn't want to talk to me anymore. There is nothing I can do about that."

"So, what? You just give up? That is not at all like you, Derrick. You usually fight to the bitter end."

His green eyes blazed with anger. "Oh, it's not over—not by a long shot. But right now I have a more important matter at hand."

"What's more important that reconciling with Noelle?"

"Finding out how this happened in the first place."

Camille leaned forward to get a closer look at him. "Derrick...what are you up to?"

"This thing stinks, Camille. Something is not right here. The reporter who broke the story said that he was given the tip that Love Unlimited was a high-class brothel by a reliable source he'd used many times."

"Who is this reliable source?"

"He wouldn't say...not even at the cost of his job."

Her forehead crinkled. "What do you mean even at the cost of his job? Derrick, say you didn't—"

His glance was enough to stop the remark. Apparently, whatever she read in his eyes answered the question for her.

"I don't see how this is helping anything. Noelle said that since there was no evidence of any solicitation, the police have stopped their investigation. All she is concerned with now is the bad media coverage she's received over the past week. That's where her focus is and where yours should be. Helping her recover from that."

Derrick frowned thoughtfully. "Noelle said?" He turned on the seat to look at her.

"You've talked to her?"

Camille immediately realized her mistake. She sighed in defeat. "Yes. She dropped by the hospital yesterday to say hello."

"Why didn't you tell me?"

"She asked me not to."

The pair rode quietly for the next several miles, before Camille finally broke the silence. "Derrick, I'm sorry. I was trying to respect her wishes, but she's as miserable as you are. The whole time she was in my room, she kept watching the door nervously. I thought about telling you, but I just didn't know."

Derrick stared out the window at the passing traffic, his mind trying to process all that had happened over the past few days. "It's okay," he muttered. "You were just doing what you thought best."

"You've got to find a way to talk to her."

"I know, Camille, I know."

The rest of the ride was silent. Derrick could only assume Camille was as lost for words as he was. In less than a week, the most promising period of his life had spontaneously combusted.

He'd found the woman of his dreams, only to end up standing by helplessly watching as her dreams fell apart. He'd come too damn close to losing his dearest friend.

And the internal battle raging in his soul between the beast that had always dwelled there and the new man that Noelle was forming with her love and affection was threatening to tear him apart.

* * *

The next day, Derrick was working in his office when the call he'd been waiting for finally came.

He answered his private line, his attention still mostly focused on the drawings laid out on the desk before him. "Hello?"

"Derrick, it's Noelle. Do you have a minute to talk?"

Derrick spun away from the drawings at the first word, instantly recognizing the voice. "How are you? Are you home? Can I come over?"

"Derrick, please, just listen." Her voice was cold, containing none of the warmth and comfort he'd expected to hear when she finally called. "I'm contacting all my clients and asking that they appear at a press conference with me the day after tomorrow. Would you be willing to do that?"

"So, is that what I am now, a client?"

She was silent for so long, he wondered if the line had dropped. "Noelle?"

"Derrick, I don't have the mental fortitude to have this conversation with you right now. At the moment, I'm too busy trying to save my business. Will you participate in the press conference or not?"

"Can I see you?"

"Never mi—"

"Yes, of course, I'll be there. When and where?"

He wrote down the place and time and tried to get her to talk to him about how she was dealing with it all, but it proved pointless. Once she had his commitment to appear at the press conference, she quickly ended the call.

Derrick spent most of the afternoon replaying the brief conversation in his head and trying to decipher any hidden messages. Trying to decide what he should do next. Trying to come to a reasonable, rational conclusion. In the end, he did what he'd always done. He listened to the little voice in his head.

Some people called it instinct, some people called it intuition, he knew in his heart of hearts it was the voice of God guiding and directing his life, as He had always done.

Even as a young boy alone in the world, the voice had been his constant companion, helping him to avoid trouble and situations that could've taken his life in a totally different direction. The voice was what had sent him into that ladies' room all those years ago and straight into the life of Camille Massey. The voice had never failed him, and he knew it never would.

A few minutes later, he had his jacket on and was headed out the door. All the confusion and uncertainty of the past week had been crystallized into a pure and clearly defined objective. As he passed Marjorie's desk in the outer office, she called out to him.

"Mr. Brandt, a Mr. Warner is on the line. Would you like me to take a message?"

"No," he called over his shoulder, "just transfer him to my cell."

By the time he reached his car, Derrick's clearly defined objective had changed.

He had a new mission.

Noelle spent the afternoon calling all her clients, and more than half agreed to appear at the press conference with her. Especially those that were now happily married as a result of her matches.

She'd also discovered to her distress that quite a few believed the stories they read in the press and no longer wanted to do business with her. It was an early indication of just how widespread the bad publicity had been.

Still, all in all, she was confident that she could weather the storm. Of course, things would never be the way they were, but she was used to looking for the silver lining.

Throughout the day, her mind kept returning to Derrick and the first call of the day. She'd intentionally made him the first call because she knew he would be the one to most rattle her composure and she thought it would be best to get him out of the way early. The problem was that instead of getting him out of the way, he'd persisted in staying with her all day.

How she'd enjoyed listening to his brandy-smooth voice—too much so. She missed him; there was no point in lying to herself. She missed everything about him. His touch, his taste, his smell. The fire and ice in those gorgeous eyes. The weight of his body in the dark of the night. The feel of his strong arms surrounding her as they snuggled under the covers together watching movies.

She felt the water forming in her eyes for the hundredth time, and the sorrow that quickly followed. She'd cried more since that man entered her life than she had in a lifetime. It was as if he'd opened some kind of emotional dam in her soul, and she had no idea as to how to close it.

But she had to. For her own sake. She should've known from the start that she was no match for Derrick Brandt. The man was like a walking, talking hurricane, and everywhere he went he left chaos in his wake. It was why the press loved him. He was a reliable source of news and entertainment, and now that hurricane effect had washed over her world and left only shattered remnants and debris of a once-promising life.

Her agency was destroyed and her heart was broken…just as she'd known it would be…and she had no one to blame but herself. And for what? Terrific sex and companionship?

No, she had to be fair. There was more to it than that. Much more. They had connected in a way the matchmaker in her would've never imagined. Two more different people could not exist, and yet somehow they'd found common ground.

Just as she was certain they had something stronger than a mutual attraction, she was still uncertain of what kind of future they could have together.

Because the fact of the matter was, Derrick was Derrick. Possessive and emotional, and demanding. That was probably never going to change.

She would always be Noelle. Sound, sensible and self-possessed. She liked who she was and had no desire to change. Not that Derrick had ever made that request.

But the ultimate question was, could oil and water occupy the same space?

No.

One would eventually have to give ground to the other. And in a union between her and Derrick, Noelle had a sneaky suspicion as to who would be giving ground.

As they had more than once in the past few days, Kimber's words came back to her. *"Noelle, pain is a part of life. You can't get around it. You just have to decide what is and is not worth the hurt."*

Was a lifetime of loving Derrick Brandt worth the hurt that would inevitably come along with it? Or more important, would the pain of living without him be even greater?

Chapter 27

Derrick stood outside the decrepit apartment building, waiting for her to come out. He knew the apartment number he was looking for but ignored the panel of buttons that buzzed the individual apartments. He did not want the person he was looking for to know he was coming.

He pulled his leather jacket tighter around him, trying to shield himself against the wind. The sun was shining, but it did little to deflect the cool winter air blowing against his body.

He glanced around the blighted neighborhood of boarded up shops and empty lots that lined the opposite side of the street. He knew this neighborhood well.

His first apartment had been just a couple of blocks away from where he was standing, the small apartment he'd shared with Chris. The two students had found each other through a posting Camille found at the school. They'd lived in prickly harmony until the day he came home early from class and found his fiancée, Anita, in bed with Chris. It was the first big betrayal of his life. Thankfully, he'd saved up enough to get his own apartment after that.

As it had more than once over the past few days, his mind wandered to Royce Massey.

On the ride over here, he'd considered how Royce would've handled this matter, and he knew it would've been a more tactful approach. Why use a cudgel when a scalpel was required?

He'd wait for the opportunity to present itself, and it would. He would get the information he needed with limited uproar and then be able to return to his first task.

A couple of minutes later, the door opened as a couple came out. They were so engrossed in their own conversation they never looked at the man standing behind the door who held on to it when they released it.

Derrick slipped inside the building and was not surprised to find the elevator was out of order. With a sigh, he began to climb the four flights of stairs that led to the apartment he was looking for.

The next day at the press conference, Noelle waited behind the curtains for her clients to arrive. She kept peeking out at the growing audience of media people. Reporters, cameramen and even a few curiosity seekers had shown to hear the formal announcement and get their first clear view of the woman at the center of a scandal that, despite the police's lack of interest, several still believed could contain some truth, if only because of the old adage of smoke and fire.

Exactly on the hour, the group of close to sixty people moved out onto the stage, crowding together to give a united front. Many had prepared statements and some spoke spontaneously, each giving their own account of the role Love Unlimited had played in their lives. After the attorney finished speaking, Derrick strode to the stage and announced he wanted to make some remarks. *When did he get here? I didn't even know he'd arrived.* Noelle felt a tickling feeling in the pit of her stomach. Derrick Brandt and the media did not mix well.

She had no idea what he wanted to say, and unfortunately, he had not bothered to bounce the idea off of her first. She said a silent prayer.

Lifting the mic to a comfortable height, Derrick looked out across the partially filled room, where reporters waited with anticipation in their eyes. She knew what they expected. Derrick Brandt was always good for a sensational story.

"As many of you know," he began, "I have not been very successful in relationships. So, a few months ago, a friend of mine suggested I try this new agency called Love Unlimited because of their unusual record of success.

"When I went for that first appointment, I did not know what to expect. Noelle's professionalism and detailed process soon put me at ease. She assured me that she would be able to find someone compatible for me in her large database of clients using a process that combined several methods. I was doubtful, as I'm sure any of you who know me would've been."

The comment brought a little laughter as Derrick joked about his own poor dating history.

"Over the process of trying to find me a compatible match, I found myself falling in love with Noelle. And just so we're clear—it was not an affection she sought or welcomed." He glanced back at her over his shoulder. "But I couldn't help the way I felt."

He returned to the audience. "During the process of sending me on dates, I was matched with a particular woman, whom I will not name here. But since we'll be filing a lawsuit for slander, her name will soon become a part of the public record. This person and I went on one date, one single encounter that consisted of dinner and nothing more. After I started dating Noelle, this other woman apparently felt some animosity and began the rumor that Love Unlimited was a escort service providing call girls."

He leaned forward over the podium. "I just want to make it perfectly clear that all of this is the result of one woman who felt she had been scorned by me. Not because of anything Noelle Brown has ever done. She has dedicated her life to helping people find and grow healthy romantic relationships. First as a relationship counselor and then as the owner of Love Unlimited. She doesn't deserve any of this."

He looked into her eyes and Noelle felt like they were the only two people in the world. Her heart soared. The group of photographers snapping shots and reporters listening with rapt attention no longer existed. "Noelle, I just wanted to say that I am so sorry that the good name of your matchmaking service has been dragged through the court of public opinion as a result of my actions. But I can't regret it, because if I'd never come to Love Unlimited, I would've never met you, and I don't even want to imagine what my life would've been like if I'd never found you."

Not caring who was there to witness it, right there on stage, Noelle reached up and wrapped her arms around Derrick's neck tightly, hugging him close. She knew that no matter what tomorrow would put before them, no matter how incompatible they might be on paper, despite the mathematical improbabilities *they would make it* simply because the sum of their love was stronger than any equation known to man.

It was well after nine that evening when Noelle and Derrick pulled up in front of her brownstone. As she put the car in Park and turned off the ignition, she asked, "Who? Why?" They'd barely been able to talk at the press conference.

"Belinda Foster."

"Belinda?" she asked in wide-eyed amazement. "One of your early dates? The *vet?* Why would she do this to me?"

Derrick quickly looked away, unable to look her in the eyes as he confessed the rest of what he'd discovered. "Me."

"Oh, my God, when you said that you did not *hit it off* with her, I didn't think anything more of it at the time, but what does that mean? What exactly happened on your date with her, Derrick? What did you say to her?"

"Hold up, before you get too high and mighty." He held up a hand defensively. "It wasn't my date with *her* that was the problem. It was my dates with *you.*"

"Your dates with me?" She tilted her head in confusion. "I don't understand."

"She saw one of the photos of us together in the paper and took offense to it."

Noelle closed her eyes as understanding finally sunk in. "She thought I was trying to steal you away from her."

"Apparently," Derrick said.

"Let's talk about this inside." She got out of the car, went up the walk and started up the stairs with Derrick on her heels.

Once they were safely behind closed doors, she picked up where they'd left off.

They kissed and kissed, barely coming up for air.

"How did you find this out?" Her mind was still having a hard time processing the fact that this had been done to her by one of her own clients. Whom she'd thought was one of her more loyal clients.

"I backtracked from the reporter who broke the story. He said he had a reliable source whom he would not divulge. So I had a P.I. follow him, assuming he would meet with the source again, and he did. The P.I. traced the individual back to an apartment building in Germantown, and when I went there today, I found the source— a guy named Diego McCarthy sharing an apartment with his cousin, Belinda."

Noelle stood stunned as he rattled off the details of his investigation. While she'd been moping and griping about his lack of support during the whole fiasco of the past week, he'd been secretly unraveling it in a way that had not even occurred to her. She'd been so busy trying to put out the fire, she'd never stopped to consider what may have started it in the first place.

"I, um, don't know what to say," she admitted. "I had no idea you were doing this. Thank you."

"It's no big deal." He shrugged. "I just needed to keep

busy. With Camille in the hospital and you…well, I just needed something to occupy my mind."

Her mind wandered.

"Penny for your thoughts." Derrick asked, as attuned to her mood as ever.

"Just thinking about Love Unlimited."

"It's not your fault."

"That's what you say, but—"

"It's not."

"Derrick, *I'm* the one who interviewed Belinda Foster. *I'm* the one who recommended her as a candidate. *I'm* the one who should've seen that she was unstable. I've always boasted that one of the things that makes Love Unlimited superior to other agencies is our thorough screening process. And yet I completely missed this."

"We both did." Derrick kissed the top of her head. "I went out with the woman, sat across a table from her for hours, and she seemed totally okay to me."

"I was thinking, maybe I should close the agency down."

Derrick maneuvered her body so he could see her face. "Why would you do that?"

"Well, I'm just afraid…What if another Belinda Foster shows up, I miss it again and send her on a date with someone and something terrible happens as a result?"

"Noelle, how many couples have you matched?"

"Over forty," she said, unable to hide a sense of pride she always felt in that knowledge.

"And how many lunatics were in that group?"

She chuckled. "Honestly, I don't know. For all I know, half of them may be holding their spouses captive in their basements. And I'm walking around with my chest out talking about what a great matchmaker I am."

"You are a great matchmaker."

"Humph."

He pulled her closer to his body. "You *are* a great matchmaker, and keep in mind, I'm a very satisfied customer."

"Yes, there's a fair opinion." She snorted. "Straight from the mouth of my soon-to-be naked lover, ladies and gentlemen."

"I'm serious. Imagine if I had gone to a different matchmaker or dating agency. We would've never found each other." He ran his hand down the side of her face. "I would've never found my other half. That's what you do, baby. You make people whole. That's important, and you have a gift for it. You can't close the agency. There are too many people out there who will never find their other halves without you."

If she had not loved the man before, that vote of confidence would've done it.

"I'll tell you what—my first call in the morning is to my lawyer to sue Belinda for libel *and* slander!"

Noelle watched as he walked to the kitchen entrance and looked in, and then walked across the hall to the living room and looked around in there.

"What are you looking for?" she asked.

After a while, he turned toward her and the sadness in his eyes melted her heart.

"You," he finally said. "I've missed being here, among your things, this place that feels like you because every room is filled with parts of you. The books you love—" he gestured to the large bookcase in the living room "—the movies you like, your favorite colors, the causes you believe in." He nodded to the wall hanging she'd bought from an animal-rights society she supported that was hanging on the hallway wall.

He looked back toward her bedroom. "I just wanted to soak up every little bit of you."

Noelle felt her heart speed up at yet another confession.

"It's okay." The corner of his mouth turned up in a small smile. "It's okay. You don't have to say anything. I know your mind must be spinning. I can't even imagine how you must feel watching Love Unlimited and all your hard work being dragged through the mud like that." He braced his body against the wall, folding his arms across his chest. "When I came over here that first time, I was fully prepared to use every seductive trick in my bag to lure you to bed. I knew I could. I know you enjoy our lovemaking as much as I do. I was convinced I could make you want me. But while I was sitting there, it hit me. Something Camille has been trying to tell me for years." He smiled. "Wise old Camille—even after all these years she still has things to teach me. She used to say that sometimes to have what you *really* want, you have to make a choice to defend it, to cherish it, to fight for it. But to do all that for the *right* kind of love."

He looked at her then and Noelle felt the intensity of his stare from the top of her head to the bottoms of her feet.

"That's it, isn't it?" He stood and headed toward the door. "I thought it was the satisfaction of being your lover, holding you in my arms and seeing your smile, but that's not it. All those things were just symbolic representations of what I really wanted." He opened the front door and turned to look at her over his shoulder.

"It's your love I wanted, Noelle. That's what I really wanted. Your unconditional love and acceptance."

"You have it!" she blurted out, and he stopped in midstep. "You already have my love."

He stepped back inside and closed the door, leaning his long body against it.

"Your had it for a long time, Derrick."

He stood still as a statue watching her.

"I've been in love with you since the moment you walked into my office the first time. And it frightens me because you're all wrong! I don't mean that in a bad way. It's just, you're not at all what I would've chosen for myself." She rubbed at her throbbing temple. "You're a lot more work that I would've liked."

For some reason that statement brought a smile to his lips. "The feeling's mutual."

"I'm not a risk taker, Derrick. And you're *all* risk."

"Love always is, Noelle. But for the winners…" His eyes closed as he imagined some secret bliss.

"But that's the problem. We don't know we'll win."

His eyes opened and he focused on her face. "Are you kidding? You and me? How could we lose?"

He sounded so certain and sure, Noelle wanted to believe him. A thought occurred to her, and she immediately pepped up at the idea. "I would feel a lot better if you'd allow me to run a comparative analysis of our profiles."

Seeing she was serious, he shook his head emphatically. "No, Noelle, just this once, none of your matchmaking mojo. Not this time. Not with us. This is not about compatibility. It's about two people who love each other. You're gonna have to roll the dice—right here, right now—and live with the consequences."

Apparently, he read her answer in her eyes, because his smile widened and he moved away from the door, slowly crossing to come to a stop directly in front of her.

"Marry me," he whispered, standing so close his breath lifted a few strands of hair on her forehead. "Marry me and you won't even have to change those monogrammed towels you keep in the bathroom. Brown, Brandt, see? There's all kinds of advantages to being my wife."

She laughed at his silliness.

"Marry me, Noelle…please."

Unable to hold back any longer, Noelle reached up and wrapped her arms around his neck, bringing his mouth down to hers. She lifted her head and smiled with tear-filled eyes. "Yes, I'll marry you, you trouble-some, temperamental man, yes, yes, yes."

Derrick pulled her body against his, having gotten the answer he wanted, and with an ease that always surprised her, he lifted her in his strong arms and carried her down the hall to her bedroom.

Derrick stood beside the bed, just holding Noelle in his arms and kissing her. Almost afraid to put her down and lose the closeness of their bodies. It had been so long since he'd held her like this, with her soft arms wound around his neck, her hardened nipples pressed against his chest, her beating heart next to his.

Slowly, careful not to break their connection, he lowered her to the bed, bringing his heavy weight on top of her, covering her body with his. She felt even better than he remembered. All sweet-smelling, soft, trembling woman.

"I love you, Noelle," he couldn't stop the words from rolling off his tongue, he wanted to make sure she understood that this was more than just lovemaking. This was something bigger and more significant. She was his now, and would always be.

"I love you, Derrick," she whispered against his neck, even as her fingers roamed across his back.

Suddenly, he wanted nothing between them. Not a stitch of clothing or cover. Just flesh against flesh. He lifted the lightweight sweater over her head, and found himself mesmerized by her full breasts pushed together by the underwire bra.

He smiled to himself. *All mine.*

As he reached to release the front latch and the bra came undone, Derrick could see that Noelle was not the only one trembling. Eager to have what had been denied to him too long, he flicked her taut nipple with his tongue, before suckling a breast into his mouth.

As expected, Noelle's whole body arched in his hands, and Derrick reveled in the knowledge that he knew her so well. He knew that he could touch her anywhere, any part of her body and predict her reaction, because she responded to him so magnificently.

How could they lose? He thought again, plundering one succulent fruit, before moving to the other. *How could this be anything but right?* Bracing her body with his large hands on her lower back, he feasted over each of her wonderful breasts, running his tongue over the contours and curves. He lavished attention on each one, letting each hardened nipple pop out of his mouth when he had his fill. She was incredibly made, everything about her was right.

He ran his hand along her backside, pulling her leg up over his hip. Just to prove he could, he ran his finger along the crease at the back of her knee, and as if on cue she moaned against his shoulder. *Perfect.*

He heard the clinking noise of his belt as Noelle worked to release it. A second later, her small hand was stroking the outline of his erection through his slacks, and then the zipper was being lowered.

Derrick fell back against the bed as her fingers closed around the object of her search. He wanted to speak, to tell her to slow down, but he found he could not speak, as she slowly stroked his manhood up and down, up and down. Her complete attention was focused on the task. She bent down to take all of him into her mouth. To lick him up and down, up and down.

Unable to form words, he covered her hand with his to stop the motion. Noelle looked at him then and all he could manage was the shake of his head, but it was enough, she understood.

She climbed to her knees and began to undo the button front flap of her own dress pants, as Derrick lay paralyzed with need. Waiting, watching as she lowered the pants and underwear down her legs, revealing herself before his eyes. She slipped both legs out of the pants and tossed them aside, crawling back across the bed to him on her knees. When she approached him, planning to lower herself into his lap, Derrick sat up and pulled her forward until he could bury his face in the curly V-shape of her body.

Noelle held on to his head with both hands, trying to fight back the mounting climax that came on so strong it stunned her. "Oh, Derrick…Derrick, I can't, I can't."

Using one hand to steady her, and the other to pull her feminine lips apart, Derrick dove in tongue first, lapping hungrily at her clitoris. He rubbed it, tongued it, flicking and softly biting it until she was spasming uncontrollably around him. Her hips undulated in front of him.

"You're so wet, Noelle," he said, lust in his raspy voice.

He ignored the slight pull on his short hair as she held on to his head and gave herself over to the release. Finally, she collapsed over his shoulder. "Oh, Derrick."

Derrick gently lowered her body onto the bed and finished removing his own pants and shirt before rejoining her. With her head turned to the side, and her arms thrown over her head, her full breasts beautifully splayed out right in front of him, she was so still and silent. The only motion seemed to be her beating heart lifting her breasts and chest. Derrick frowned, wondering if she'd fallen asleep. Her body stirred, and she relaxed.

She turned her head and smiled at him. "That was wonderful."

He smiled back. "You ain't seen nothing yet." He reached into her nightstand, fishing around with no luck. "Did you get rid of the condom I left in here?"

She sat up on her elbows. "When did you leave any condoms here?"

He moved off her to check the drawer more carefully. "When I brought you home after our first date." He found the small packet he'd placed in the far rear of the drawer and donned the condom.

"You said we didn't have sex that night."

"We didn't." He winked. "But I knew we would, so I wanted to be prepared."

"How could you be so presumptuous?" She laughed.

Derrick sat back on his knees with his throbbing erection standing like a flagpole between them. He gestured to the air between them. "I was right, wasn't I?"

All he wanted was to bury himself deep inside her body and stay there for the rest of the night.

He took both her hands in his, pinning her to the bed. "I love you, Noelle, and although I was sexually attracted to you from our first meeting, that night was the night I fell in love. You were so adorably tipsy, and open and wonderful, and all I wanted was to make love to you. But I couldn't...*because* you were so adorably tipsy. So, leaving the condoms was my way of staking a claim, and yes, that may sound possessive and primitive, but that's who I am—you know this. And I'm sorry if you're offended by my need to stake a claim, but you are too rare a woman for me to risk another man getting here first!"

She lay beneath him, staring up at him with smiling eyes.

"Well?" Derrick asked, trying to ignore the pain of his aching erection.

A slow smile came back across her face. "Well...are you going to sit there all day, or do you plan to do something with that." She glanced down at the deep red rod pulsating between their bodies.

Derrick lowered himself over her body, pushing into her tight, warm opening, and over the next few hours, he found several ways to show her exactly what he could do with *that*.

Derrick plunged in deep, then drew back out. He stroked her, just at the tip of her wet folds, leaving her almost begging for more...he waited...then buried himself back in her depths. Their eyes met and stayed. Noelle spread her legs, meeting every one of his fierce pumps into her own. She buried her fingernails in his back while she drew one leg up onto his shoulder.

Derrick sank deeper. Deeper than any man had ever gone. Noelle didn't even stifle her moans as she submitted to him, riding the waves of ecstasy as she came again and again.

Afterwards, Derrick held her, stroking her hair. "So no more talk about closing down Love Unlimited?"

She sighed, jolted back to reality. Despite Derrick's encouraging words earlier, she knew keeping the agency open would be the equivalent of starting from scratch. After the way the press had savaged her reputation, she would have to rebuild from the ground up.

"It won't be easy."

"Nothing worth doing ever is."

"I lost a lot of clients."

"And you'll get some more. You'll tell everyone who comes to your office our story—hell, even Camille's story—and bring out your colorful brochures, and before you know it, you'll be back on track."

"How is she, by the way?"

"The doctor says with the pacemaker and retirement she's going to be fine."

"Oh, thank God."

"But you and Love Unlimited will be back in no time. Just watch."

"Will you always remind me of all that when I get discouraged and need a little boost? In work and in life?"

"Always."

As Noelle looked into the passionate, private man's beautiful eyes, and glimpsed—like she had that very first time—what was beneath the public facade, Noelle knew in her very soul that he always would.

He revealed the Braddock's
most scandalous secret…

The Object of His Protection

New York Times bestselling author

BRENDA JACKSON

Investigator Drey St. John's discovery that Senator Braddock
was his father drives him to uncover the truth behind his
death. He needs forensic scientist Charlene Anderson's
help…but their simmering mutual attraction
complicates *everything*.

THE BRADDOCKS

SECRET SON

power, passion and politics are all in the family

Available the first week of November wherever books are sold.

KIMANI™
ROMANCE

KPBJ0881108

Win, lose…or surrender!

The player's proposal
angie daniels

Danica Danforth's sizzling affair with
Jaden Beaumont left her feeling the fool.
Then fate reunited them when her car broke
down, stranding her in Jaden's body shop.
Now Jaden was determined to find out why
she'd left him, and just what game she was
playing. Because his heart was in this for real.

*Available the first week of November
wherever books are sold.*

KIMANI
ROMANCE
™

www.kimanipress.com

KPAD0901108

She was a knockout!

Love**TKO**
pamela yaye

Boxer Rashawn Bishop woos stunning
Yasmin Ohaji with finesse and fancy footwork,
and finally TKO's her resistance. But love means
making choices, and with his career on the line,
will he follow the lure of boxing…or the woman
he can't live without?

"A fun and lighthearted story."
—Romantic Times BOOKreviews
on Pamela Yaye's *Other People's Business*

*Available the first week of November
wherever books are sold.*

KIMANI™
ROMANCE

www.kimanipress.com

KPPY0911108

**Breaking up is hard to do…
even when you know it's right.**

NATIONAL BESTSELLING AUTHOR

marcia
King-
Gamble

first crush

Hudson Godfrey's new wine-making business leaves
him with no time for a relationship, so he breaks up with
one-of-a-kind woman Laila Stewart. Of course, he didn't
realize she would wind up moving to Washington state
and working with him. Or that their heated daytime
glances would lead to sizzling passionate nights. Now
he's starting to wonder if letting this alluring woman go
was the biggest mistake of his life….

*Coming the first wefi of November 2008,
wherever books are sold.*

ARABESQUE®

www.kimanipress.com

"A delightful book romance lovers will enjoy."
—*Romantic Times BOOKreviews*
on *Love Me or Leave Me*

ESSENCE BESTSELLING AUTHOR

GWYNNE FORSTER

Secret desire

Their lives spared but nerves shattered in a
harrowing robbery, independent widow
Kate Middleton and her young son are rescued
by Luke Hickson, a handsome police captain still
reeling from a calamity of his own. Neither Kate nor
Luke expects, much less welcomes, their instant
attraction. But when trouble strikes again, Kate
realizes there's only one place she feels safe—
in Luke's strong embrace.

*Coming the first wefi of November 2008,
wherever books are sold.*

ARABESQUE®

www.kimanipress.com

KPGFI141108

ESSENCE BESTSELLING AUTHOR

DONNA HILL

Temptation

Liaisons, Noelle Maxwell's chic romantic retreat, is the ultimate fantasy. But there is no idyllic escape from her past, and Noelle has vowed to uncover the truth behind the mysterious death of her husband. Yet the only man she can trust is a stranger whose explosive sexuality awakens desire—and fear. Because Cole Richards has a secret, too....

"Riveting and poignant, this novel will transport readers to new heights of literary excellence."
**—*Romantic Times BOOKreviews*
on *Temptation***

Coming the first week of October wherever books are sold.

ARABESQUE®

www.kimanipress.com

KPDHI081008